John Blessington's Enemy

A Story of Life in South Africa

POST CARD

Correspondence   Address

"THE BOY FLUNG THE LIQUID OVER JOHN BLESSINGTON." (*p.* 83.)

John Blessington's Enemy

A Story of Life in South Africa

By

E. Harcourt Burrage

Author of "The Missing Million," "Gerard Mastyn,"
etc., etc.

WITH SIX ILLUSTRATIONS

London

S. W. Partridge & Co.

8 and 9 Paternoster Row

CONTENTS.

CHAPTER I.

CHAPTER X.

CHAPTER XI.

CHAPTER XII.

John Blessington's Enemy

CHAPTER I.

NEIGHBOURS IN NAME ONLY.

A FRESH-COMPLEXIONED, pleasant-looking woman of about fifty years of age stood by the door of a big, rambling wooden house, shading her eyes with her hand from the light of the setting sun, and gazing anxiously across a wide stretch of land, known in the Transvaal as the Jugersdorf region.

Within a radius of her, comprising about two hundred acres of land, the hand of the cultivator was in evidence. There were no fields as we know them in England, but there were nevertheless portions of the farm of John Blessington clearly defined by broad burrows and footpaths, set out for the regular cultivation of various crops in due season. At the time of our story the corn was ripening, and it was the wife of the farmer, John Blessington, who was looking across the charming spread of golden grain towards an irregular and somewhat barren tract of land beyond. Her mind was busy with apprehension concerning her two sons, who had left early that morning to shoot in a distant kopje.

"I don't see them coming, John," she said, "and it will shortly be dark."

"They will be coming along home soon," answered a cheery voice from within the house.

"Ah, John!" sighed Mrs. Blessington, "you are more trustful of the Karders than I am. They would do you or the boys mischief at any time, if it could be done in safety. They want to see us out of here. Hans Karder has set his heart on getting the Golden Farm from you."

A tall, broad-shouldered man, fair-haired and frank of countenance, of about the same age as the woman, came out of the shadows of the house, and stood in the sunlight by her side.

"Hans Karder," he said, with a smile, "can have the Golden Farm at my price, but not for the sum he offers."

"Why did he take to Barren Lands Farm?" asked Mrs. Blessington.

"Because there are a thousand acres of it," said John Blessington, "with big kopjes around where the gemsbok and other game used to be plentiful enough. But he has shot them all, with the help of his son, and now he has turned to steady work he finds his land isn't worth much. I think I'll go across as far as the Big Spring. The boys may be bathing in the pool near it. They've a wholesome love for cold water, inside and out."

He walked away, and the woman turned into the house. Everywhere there were indications of its being a settler's home. John Blessington had built it ten years before, when he first trekked into the Jugersdorf country. He made the furniture, put up his barns and sheds for the cattle, and with such odd help as he could get, cultivated the ground until his two boys were big enough to help him.

A girl of seventeen came into the room where the mother was busy laying the cloth for supper. It was Polly, the eldest child, and only daughter of the Blessingtons.

"We cannot have supper yet," said Mrs. Blessington, quietly; "the boys are very late to-night, and father's gone to look for them."

Polly was very pretty, and, what is of more value than mere charm of face and figure, had abounding health, resulting from an active and mainly outdoor life.

In a little while the sun went down, and darkness fell upon the land. The stars came out, brilliantly gleaming, but there was no moon to give the stronger light that would have been of real service to mother and daughter as they made frequent trips to the door and with growing apprehension surveyed the darkened landscape.

At last, as Mrs. Blessington stood at the door, with Polly peering over her shoulder, a flash of light about a mile away suddenly relieved the gloom. It was gone in a moment, and in a few seconds the report of a gun was heard. Then there was a second flash and another report; and Polly, trembling, threw her arms around her mother.

"Don't be alarmed, my child," urged Mrs. Blessington. "It may be nothing more than your father scaring off some of Karder's cattle from the corn. He's a neighbour in name only, and sets them straying at night on purpose to feed on our crops."

A few minutes later mother and daughter heard the sound of someone coming along one of the paths between the corn and mangel patches, and quickly recognised John Blessington's familiar footstep. There was no accompanying tread of other feet, and their anxious fears increased. The farmer, walking as one weary, hove in sight and motioned for them to go in. He followed and closed the door.

"The boys are not at the pool," he said. "They may have shot a gemsbok in the kopje and have stopped to skin and cut it up."

"Was there a gemsbok by the corn patch?" asked Mrs. Blessington.

"No. It was something else—I could not be sure what," he answered quietly. "Have your supper and go to bed, Polly."

They ate their frugal meal of brown bread, butter, and cheese. Water was their only drink, and the girl, who had been silently watching her father's thoughtful face with wondering eyes, presently rose from the table, kissed her parents, and with a sigh stole softly away to her room.

"John," said Mrs. Blessington, "you can tell me now what you fired at."

"I didn't fire at anything," he answered; "but somebody fired at *me*."

"You are sure of that, John?"

"The shots whistled close to my head, and I fear it couldn't have been an accidental thing. Never mind that now. It's the boys that I'm worrying about."

He was a strong man both in mind and body. Having from his youth led a sober life, he generally had the nerve to bear perturbing matters with outward composure, but he showed signs of giving way now.

He bowed his head, and a choking sob escaped him. Then there was a silence that lasted a minute or more, to be broken by a hurried footstep outside. John Blessington sprang to his feet.

"God help us, Mary!" he gasped. "Whoever it is, there is only *one*, and we are groaning in our hearts for *two*."

CHAPTER II.

A VERY DOUBTFUL LANDSLIP.

THE door was thrown open, and a big, burly man with a heavily bearded face came in. He was of about the same age as John Blessington, but of coarser build. The only thing small about him were his eyes, which lay deep in his head, and were further hidden by a habit he had of puckering his face as if he stood in a light too strong for his vision. He wore the shirt, breeches, boots, and hat of the Boer farmer.

"I've come along quick, neighbour," he said, in deep guttural accents, with a broad Boer twang, "to bring ye bitter news."

"Let me know what it is," replied John Blessington; "don't beat about the bush. The wife and I are strong people in the time of sorrow."

"Your boys were in a cave in the kopje," said the visitor, "when the land slipped and buried both alive."

Mrs. Blessington dropped helplessly into a

chair.   Her husband stood like a figure of marble, with a white face turned towards the Boer.

"You couldn't have brought me more bitter news than that, Hans Karder," he said.   His voice was husky, and his eyes dim with rising tears.   "How came you to know of it?"

"My Jan came home with the news," answered the Boer; "he saw it.   Your boys were too proud-stomached to heed his warning.   Jan knew the place was dangerous."

"Where is he now?"

"By the barns, holding our horses."

"I'll be gone to the kopje and see what can be done," said John Blessington, wearily. "Ye'll show me the way to the cave, may be?"

"Aye, neighbour, and help ye to dig out the poor lads," said Hans Karder, puckering his face so that his eyes were almost invisible.

Polly must have been listening outside.   At all events she had not gone to bed, for now she glided into the room fully dressed.   "I'll look to mother," she said, softly.   The quiet calmness of the girl was amazing.

John Blessington gave his wife a kiss, and she mutely responded with another, and a glance from her eyes, full of that deep woe which finds no adequate expression in words.

"'WE'VE BEEN GETTING A FEW ROUGH CHARACTERS IN
JUGERSDORF, NEIGHBOUR,' HE SAID." (*p.* 17.)

The two men left the house, and in an adjoining shed John Blessington found and lighted a lantern. In the corner were tools for digging, and he selected what were requisite.

The next thing he sought was his horse, which he quickly saddled, and with Hans Karder joined a tall, raw-boned youth, who stood near one of the barns, holding two other impatient horses by their bridles. The digging tools were divided, and to each rider a spade and pick were apportioned.

It was impossible to ride quickly over that rough country in the dark. Perforce they had to pick their way, which enabled Hans Karder to open a conversation.

"We've been getting a few rough characters in Jugersdorf, neighbour," he said.

"Aye, aye," replied John Blessington, absently. "How's that? I've not seen 'em."

"They calls themselves prospectors," said Hans Karder; "but their business is robbery and murder, to my thinking. Two or three of them have called at my house this evening, but I bid 'em begone."

"That's not the old hospitality," said John Blessington. "We've never yet turned a going-up man from our door."

"Ye were always trustful, neighbour," said

B

Hans Karder, with a smile. "I thought some of the lot might have come to the Golden Farm."

"I'm thinking of my boys," said John Blessington, pathetically, and the subject dropped.

Guided by Jan, at last they reached the kopje. There they dismounted, and having secured their animals, took their picks and spades, and journeyed to the scene of the disaster. A waning moon was now rising above the horizon, and there was light enough to work by.

The landslip was not far away, nor was it of sufficient size to have attracted special notice until it was pointed out. A rock had rolled down a slope, and the earth above had followed, burying up and crushing in a small cave.

"It wasn't more than big enough to stable a couple of cows," said Hans.

John Blessington gave him no answer, but, throwing off his coat, began energetically to work with pick and spade. The two Boers, in a more leisurely way, lent their aid. Hans Karder, before starting, produced a big flask and took a sip from it. An offer to John Blessington to share in the drink was declined with a shrug of the shoulders. So the flask was passed to Jan, who showed he was nowise averse to partaking of the fiery schnapps.

For every spadeful thrown aside by the Boers.

John Blessington cast three. In addition to his natural strength and powers of endurance, he was inspired by his fatherly anxiety. He worked on one side of the fallen mass, the two Boers laboured on the other. In a little while a small hole appeared where the Englishman was working. He stooped, putting his mouth to the opening, and cried hoarsely, " My boys, are you there ? "

" Yes," answered a faint voice, " but I'm afraid poor Joe is gone."

It was a sight to see how John Blessington worked then. He threw aside the earth and stones as so much water, until there was an opening big enough for him to creep through. But a few seconds elapsed ere he reappeared, with the still form of a boy of fourteen in his arms. Behind him tottered another lad, about a year older.

A short distance away was a spring. The father, sobbing almost hysterically under the stress of his emotion, carefully laid his burden down upon the ground, and with his hands tossed the cool liquid upon the boy's face. The elder son looked to himself.

Jan and his father stood by, looking on and doing nothing. Sam, the elder boy, having recovered from his exhaustion sufficiently to speak, pointed a denunciatory finger at the younger Boer and said :

"It was you who loosened the boulder, Jan, and it was a cowardly, cruel thing to do!"

"I fetched your father to you," roared Jan, evading a direct reply to the accusation.

"Quiet there!" cried John Blessington. "I think my poor boy Joe is speaking to me."

They stood still in obedience to his almost fierce request, and he bent over poor Joe, with his ear close to the mouth of the boy. But neither word nor sign came from the parted lips to relieve his overwhelming anxiety

CHAPTER III.

A VERY TRYING ENCOUNTER.

It seemed as if poor Joe were really dead, and John Blessington wept as strong men weep—silently. But Sam had the hopefulness of youth in his heart. Kneeling down beside his brother, he rubbed his hands vigorously, and asked his father to lave the boy's forehead with the cool water of the spring. The result of these efforts was that presently Joe's eyelids were seen to quiver, and there was a slight movement of the lips. Hopefully they laboured on, and soon had the gratification of hearing him softly sigh.

The worst was over. Endowed with the sound constitution that comes of healthful, temperate living, Joe soon recovered sufficiently to sit up and drink a little water. Hans Karder derisively offered his beloved flask in vain, and ostentatiously emptied it himself, with the air of a man who had a superior knowledge of what was good to drink.

Joe was put upon the horse, and his father led

21

it home, with Sam walking beside his brother. The Boer and his boy Jan went off with a curt "Good-night," as if they were disappointed with the results of the evening's work.

Sam explained all that had happened. It was Jan, it seemed, who had pointed out the cave, and suggested searching it to see if anything of interest could be found there. He told the boys that in a similar place he had found some Kaffir spears, and so excited their curiosity. They went in, leaving Jan outside, and a few moments later the boulder came thundering down.

"It's hard to believe a mere boy could attempt to take your lives," said John Blessington, sorrowfully, "but I am afraid the Karders are an all-round bad lot. However, we will act in a Christian spirit, and try to believe they are not guilty. There is a possibility of its being an accident."

What joy there was in that little household when the party returned! A narrower escape of their lives the boys could hardly have in the future. But for the roots of some bushes, which supported the soft soil, and left them a moderate breathing space, they must have perished. As things were, they just managed to breathe and keep alive. In another hour both would have been dead.

A week passed by before they saw anything more of Jan, and then one morning, as they rode on their stout cobs over the land adjoining the farm, he came galloping up on a big, raw-boned horse.

"You've just got to keep to your own land," he said; "one of our heifers was shot yesterday and another is lamed."

"What has that to do with us?" asked Sam; "we never interfere with your cattle."

"Jan," said Joe, "you are a bad lot, I am afraid. It was you who set the big boulder rolling. I am almost as sure of it as if I'd seen it done."

Jan grinned, and drawing out a pipe, filled it with strong tobacco, and began to smoke. He blew great clouds of vapour from his mouth and assumed the air of an elder and superior. It occurred to Sam that he looked something like an ape, mimicking the ways of men.

"When *I* am master here," he said, "you will have to clear out. I detest you English, and I hate *you* most of all."

He touched his horse with his whip, and riding up to Sam, blew a cloud of smoke into his face. Then he gave him a backhand blow on the breast that nearly knocked the boy off his horse.

This was going too far, and Sam hit back, causing Jan to lose his balance, so that he tumbled to the ground. Being an expert rider, however, he kept hold of the reins, and so prevented his horse getting away. In a few moments he was in the saddle again, white with rage.

"Look to yourselves!" he said, threateningly, making a lunge at Sam.

For a minute or so there was a confusion of plunging and rearing, but Joe and Sam managed to keep their seats; and as soon as they could get free from Jan they rode away homeward.

"Jan is going a bit too far," said Joe, as he swished the air with his whip, locally known by the name of sjambok, with anger stamped on his face. "I shall not put up with much more of his nonsense."

"Leave him to me," returned Sam, quietly.

"That is all very well," rejoined Joe; "he insults us both. Don't forget that."

"We were two to one just now," remarked Sam, unmoved by the heat displayed by his brother, "and that stayed my hand. I don't want to give the rascal a chance of saying we attacked him unfairly."

"He's a bad specimen of his race, anyway," said Joe, shrugging his shoulders. With a crack of his sjambok he urged his horse onward, and the rest of the ride home was silently performed by the brothers.

"JAN KEPT HOLD OF THE REINS." (*p.* 24.)

There had always been a rift between the Karders and the Blessingtons, and it was rapidly widening into a gulf. Being, in a South African sense, neighbours, it was impossible entirely to avoid coming in contact with each other. The straying of cattle from one farm to the other was a matter of frequent occurrence, and one morning, a few days later, Sam found two steers belonging to Hans Karder among their own herd. He singled them out, and drove the beasts over the bordering land of the two farms, and that simple act brought him again into contact with Jan, who came riding down from a small kopje at a furious pace.

"Stop, you Sam Blessington!" he shouted; "didn't I warn you the other day to leave our cattle alone?"

Sam was disposed to ignore the young bully, but he felt it would be a course calculated to inspire him to further acts of insolence; so he reined up his horse and waited for Jan to get nearer, ere he uttered a word in response to his threatening bellowings.

Jan came on, all the more confidently because Sam was alone, and it rather surprised him to find no indication of fear in the bearing of the "young rooinek," as he on occasion termed him. Believing it was mere temporary swagger Sam was display-

ing, Jan rode up close to him and raised his
sjambok above his head.

"I've a mind to cut you across the face," he
said.

"You've a better mind not to do it," replied
Sam; "and just you hearken to me, Jan. I can
handle a sjambok as well as you and perhaps a
little better, and if it comes to using mine upon
you, I'll not leave off until you cry out for mercy."

"You! you! sjambok *me*," hissed Jan, swelling
with fury; "you rooinek! you!" He swung his
sjambok round to strike, and the lash of Sam's
whistled in the air, entwining itself with that of
the young Boer. Thus both were for the moment
rendered harmless. The two horses collided, and
Sam seizing the handle of Jan's sjambok, wrenched
it from his grasp.

"Now you can go home," cried Sam, "and I'll
keep this as a trophy of war."

Jan backed his horse a little and sat mute in
the saddle, staring at Sam for a minute or more.
Then he broke out with a passionate appeal for his
sjambok to be restored to him.

"What am I to say at home when I return
without it?" he asked.

"Whatever you please," answered Sam. "I was
doing you a kindness when you rode at me like a
ruffian; and if I had shrunk from you, as a coward

might have done, you would have beaten me as you do your poor helpless Kaffirs. I know how deep a disgrace your people think it is to have a sjambok taken away from one of you, especially by a 'rooinek,' and I don't see that I need consider your feelings in the matter. Go home and make the best of your loss."

Sam wheeled his horse round, fastened his own sjambok to the pommel of his saddle, cracked thrice the one he had taken from Jan, and rode away. Jan sat for a few moments lowering at his triumphant antagonist, with his lips quivering.

" I'll pay you back, rooinek!" he suddenly broke out, shaking both his clenched fists in the air; "and I'll have something more than a sjambok from you before I'm satisfied."

The two steers Sam had driven over the borders of the farms were browsing peacefully hard by. Jan rode at them as if they were his enemies, and indeed he felt foolishly bitter against them as the indirect authors of his humiliation. They had certainly been instrumental in leading up to an encounter Jan had been worsted in.

" Hi! hi! " he shouted.

The steers looked round at him as if they expected to see the lash of the sjambok whirling near their backs. Whether they missed it or not it is impossible to say. It is difficult for us to understand how far the power of observation goes with animals. Certain it is that they did not, as they would have done under ordinary circumstances, trot away, ahead of their driver, but moved along at a crawling pace, pausing here and there to partake of some tempting morsel of their natural food.

"The very beasts know what's happened to me," muttered Jan; and turning his horse aside from the steers he rode homeward with his head bowed upon his breast.

Meanwhile Sam had returned to the farm and was putting his horse in its stall when Joe came in. His quick eye singled out the strange sjambok, which Sam had hung upon a nail. He cast an inquiring glance at his brother.

"Jan's," said Sam, in a matter-of-fact way. "He threatened me with it, and I took it away from him."

"Well done!" cried Joe, as he gave Sam a hearty smack upon the back; "how precious small he must have felt when he got home."

"We needn't say anything about it indoors," remarked Sam; "there are other things to worry mother and father without troubling them with our quarrels with Jan. We want help for the harvest, or some of the crops will never be got in."

"We must work early and late," said Joe, "and having done our best we can do no more."

A very strange thing—strange because it was totally unexpected—happened that night. As the family sat at supper, somebody knocked at the door. John Blessington opened it and found a stranger standing there.

" I want shelter and a bit of food," he said.

" I never refuse either to a wanderer," replied John Blessington. "Come in."

The stranger took a seat at the table, and cast his hat into a corner of the room. Then he looked round at the family.

" You'll want help this harvest," he said. " I'm good for a week or more, and I'll ask nothing but food and shelter."

" Never was help more welcome," said John Blessington.

The stranger ate his supper in a somewhat uncouth fashion, such as a lonely life engenders, but he was content with his fare, and when he found there was no strong drink to be had, he simply made a wry face and said, " I'll shift with water, then." He was no great talker, and seemed to be thinking of something far away.

A bed was given him, in a room at the back of the house, and when all but the farmer and his wife had retired, this unlooked-for coming of help was brought under discussion.

"He has never worked on a farm," said Mrs. Blessington, "and I don't like his looks. Something will happen while he is here, I am sure."

"Women are ever timorous of strangers, especially if they are a bit rough in their looks," rejoined her husband. "I cannot see what will happen more than that we shall have a man working for us at a time we sorely want him, and he asks for little."

"That's what I don't like," returned Mrs. Blessington; "he is too cheap."

They went to bed eventually, and in the repose that comes to tired workers soon forgot the stranger. He was not asleep, however, but as soon as he thought he could safely do so he arose, lighted the candle in his room, took from his pocket a parcel containing some heavy substance, and laid it out on the counterpane.

CHAPTER IV.

SEEDTIME AND HARVEST.

WHATEVER it was the guest of the Blessingtons had in that small parcel, it certainly was of absorbing interest to him, for he sat up half the night examining and turning it over and over, occasionally stopping to think long and deeply, as one who has a very abstruse problem to solve. Morning was approaching when he finally put it away in his pocket, and, lying down in his clothes, dropped off to sleep.

Notwithstanding the brevity of his time of rest, he was the first up and out in the morning. John Blessington, always an early riser, found him at dawn engaged in performing his ablutions at a trough by the cattle-yard, in which half a dozen cows were awaiting the coming of Polly to milk them.

"Friend," said John, "between man and man there is nothing like a clear understanding. First of all, what is your name?"

"Ephraim Bull," replied the other. "I've borne it for forty years of a wandering life, and it will serve me to the end, I hope."

"You offer to work for me, and ask nothing more than board and lodging. That's unusual. Labour commands good pay out here."

"I'm not worth more than my food and a bed," answered Ephraim Bull, "for I'm a poor farm-worker. You must put me on the roughest jobs, and you'll find me ready and willing. And mark you, friend Blessington, I'm no scoundrel, but a true man for all my roughness. See this hand, gnarled and knotted like a bit of old oak? It's done all sorts of things in its time, but it was never raised to strike a man, without just cause or in self-defence. Not a twisted finger of the lot has been used for picking and stealing. Keep me here, ask no questions, and one day you will be thankful you trusted me."

The farmer looked at him steadily. There was the light of honesty in the man's eyes, and instinctively their hands met in a close, strong grip.

"I'll trust you as a brother," said John Blessington.

Harvest was begun that morning. The farmer and his two boys did the reaping, and Mrs. Blessington and Polly tied the sheaves. Ephraim Bull stood them up in groups for the ears of corn to dry thoroughly. He was no talker. All the day long the thoughtful, absent-minded look never left his wrinkled face.

As soon as the sun went down the tired toilers retired to rest. The next morning they were up with the dawn, and there was nothing but work, work until night came again. Glorious weather favoured them, and within a fortnight the corn was partly stacked, and the rest placed in the barn, ready to be early threshed.

The young moon had come and lay low in the heavens as the farmer, his family, and their guest sat at supper, out of doors. The night was warm, and there was no wind. During harvest time nothing had been seen of Hans Karder or Jan, which was strange, for they were usually seen almost daily near or far.

Mrs. Blessington had entertained more kindly views of Ephraim Bull after the first day or two than she did at the outset, but she could not quite make up her mind to like him. "He's too thoughtful, John," she would say to her husband, "and has something on his mind." She now turned upon the old man somewhat sharply.

"Do you know Hans Karder?" she asked, abruptly.

"I've known him off and on these twenty years," replied Ephraim Bull.

" You never told us that before."

" Well, no, ma'am, I haven't spoken of him. I'm not over and above proud of the acquaintance. But as I'm going to-night I thought I could speak out. There isn't much friendship between me and Hans Karder nowadays, though years ago we trekked together."

" John," said Mrs. Blessington, " did you know Ephraim was going to-night ? "

" No," replied the farmer, " but he can do as he pleases."

" You are a queer man," said Mrs. Blessington to Ephraim Bull, who smiled in a peculiar way, but made no reply.

Supper over, he rose and looked at the family one by one in a quiet, almost pathetic way. When he spoke his voice was husky, and his words came brokenly from his lips.

" You're a bonny family," he said, " and my stay here has made me think of a home I might have had, but I threw it away to live a careless life. I've known peace and happiness among you, and I hope one day to give you something in return. Good-bye."

He shook hands with them all, and refusing an offer to stay the night, went away across the stubble of the cornfields in the direction of Hans Karder's farm.

"A very curious sort of man," said Mrs. Blessington, shaking her head. "John, you were always too trustful."

Polly helped her mother to clear the table, and John Blessington and the boys went to have a last look at the barns and cattle-sheds. In the latter the cows were lying down, and the doors of the former they closed and made fast with a simple catch and peg of wood. In that lone region locks were rarely used for the out-buildings.

"I am too trustful, your mother says," remarked the farmer, as he turned back with the boys; "perhaps I am. It's more comforting to trust than to doubt. I think Ephraim is an honest man."

The boys slept together in a room with a window overlooking the cattle-yard. On retiring, they sat up awhile, talking of the man who had so strangely come and gone. Like their mother, they were disposed to think he had a troubled mind.

Joe was seated on a stool by a window, resting his elbows on the sill, and with his eyes fixed on the dark outline of the barns. The young moon had gone down.

"Sam," cried Joe, suddenly leaping up, "there's somebody in the cattle-yard!"

The heavy clang of the barn door being dashed to, confirmed this startling assertion, and the form of a man was dimly seen hurrying away in the direction Ephraim Bull had taken an hour earlier.

"Something's wrong," said Sam, "but stop a moment before we rouse father. What's that light? Oh, Joe, the barn is on fire!"

It was too true. From a mere spark of light there leaped up a broad sheet of flame. The corn, harvested in the barn ready for threshing, had been set alight. Ere the cries of the terrified boys had fully aroused the farmer and his wife, the interior of the wooden structure was raging like a furnace.

CHAPTER V.

A RUINED HOME.

"Fire!" There is no more awful cry wherewith to rouse a man who is peacefully sleeping. John Blessington started up in his bed and heard his boys clamouring at the door—"Father, the barn is on fire!"

Mrs. Blessington awoke, and was dazed by the terrible nature of the catastrophe. Though the window of the farmer's room looked the other way, the glare of the blazing barn was seen, lighting up the land and scattered trees with its red glow. Fire in a place which none of them ever entered with a light when corn or straw was stored there! How did it come to pass?

"Surely," groaned John Blessington, as he hurried on his clothes, "an enemy has done this."

He knew from the first he could do nothing to stave off a terrible disaster. The supply of water was poor, and he had nothing that could effectively cope with the flames. As he hurried out with his boys, he prayed in his heart that the mischief might end with the burning of the barn.

"Get out the cattle and horses!" he cried.

The gate of the stockyard was thrown open, and the scared cattle, with heads erect, came tearing out. Perforce they had to be allowed to go where they willed. Then came the turn of the horses, and they reared and plunged as the farmer and the boys led them away from the flames. The terror-inspiring effect of fire upon spirited animals renders them almost unmanageable. It required all the nerve and strength of Sam and Joe to prevent their steeds breaking away.

But if once they broke loose the chances of seeing them again were very small. So, at the risk of their lives, the brothers held on to the halters and got them away to a hollow at a distance, in which there was a shed where the calves sheltered from the rain, and where in winter-time the heifers were stabled when the weather was rough.

There the horses, having been secured to a hay-rack, were left; and as the farmer and his boys turned back they were appalled to find the fire would not be confined to the barn. The stacks of corn, though fully a hundred yards away, had caught alight. The straw was so dry

"THE SCARED CATTLE CAME TEARING OUT." (*p.* 40.)

that a spark set it going like tinder. A few faint puffs of air sufficed to fan it into a flame.

"Ruin, hopeless ruin!" muttered John Blessington, as he hurried on, opening and shutting his hands in his agony.

Nor was this the worst. Huge flakes of fire were falling in every direction. The roof of the house was speckled with them, and it was of wood, dried by the summer's heat—prepared, as one may say, for a conflagration.

Mrs. Blessington was already busy with Polly in removing things from the house. The need of saving as much as they could from their little store was too apparent. Provisions had been the first care of the housewife, and in a heap on an open space of ground, well away from the fire, boxes and packages were lying jumbled together.

In a populated country a crowd would speedily have assembled; but in that lone land not a creature came near them to help. Alone the family did their best to combat with the horror of the hour—it was no more—when swift destruction came to the house and outbuildings.

Thus swiftly the barns, cattle-sheds, and stables had been reduced to ashes. There was neither home to shelter the family, nor corn left to give them bread in the trying time of the grim, sad winter in South Africa. They had nothing but the cattle and horses, and the root crop, as yet not gathered in.

They stood together in sad silence and watched the masses of the fire until nothing but glowing ashes remained. Then John Blessington proceeded to prepare a crude shelter for his wife and daughter.

"It will be better to sleep and forget it until to-morrow," he said, grimly. "The boys and I can rest in the open air."

He rigged up with clothes and linen a passable gipsy's tent, and there mother and daughter passed the rest of the night. He and the boys slept on the mattresses, with a rug over them; and it says much for their spirit of resignation to trouble that one and all slept soundly.

Three persons appeared early in the morning— Hans Karder, his wife, and Jan. They came on foot, bringing with them a few necessaries.

"I spied your ruined house, neighbour," said Hans Karder, "as I went out this morning to drive in the cows for milking. It's a sore loss, but you are the man to bear it bravely. There's room in my house for all, till you've settled what ye'll do."

John Blessington looked at his wife, who cast a pitying glance at Polly. With no shelter for any of them, and the one waggon they possessed destroyed by the fire, what were they to do? Would it be wise to refuse such an offer, though it came from a man who had been an almost openly avowed enemy?

"Neighbour," he said, "yours is an offer such as a good man would make, and I accept it with my hearty thanks."

"Come back with me," said Hans Karder, "and leave the women and young folks to pack your things. We'll return with my waggon, and shift your goods to the shelter of Barren Lands."

Thus it was brought about that John Blessington had to take up his abode with a man who was in his heart his foe—a step that by-and-by brought matters to a climax, and changed the whole course of his life.

CHAPTER VI.

WHO DID THE DEED?

"NEIGHBOUR," said Hans Karder, as he and John Blessington walked away, "how come ye to set your place on fire?"

"It was none of our doing," answered John Blessington, in his quiet, even way of speaking; "some stranger did it. My boys saw him running away like a thief in the night."

"Ah!" rejoined Hans Karder, "ye've been entertaining a man ye know nothing of. I glimpsed him from a distance and saw he was one of the prospecting fellows. So I never come near ye, for I detest and fear the breed."

"What makes you so bitter against them? They can prospect and do no harm here. What are they seeking?"

"Gold, diamonds, minerals, the mad fools! So I reckon. But there's none of such things here. Who was the man you sheltered?"

"He gave the name of Ephraim Bull."

Hans Karder stopped and stared at John Blessington with more expression than was usually seen on his stolid face. For once in a way his eyes were open wide, and the pupils, of a dull hazel hue, dilated with unfeigned astonishment and dismay.

"So," he said, after a pause, "ye've been harbouring that black sheep?"

"He said he knew you," replied John Blessington with a sharp glance at his companion.

"It's many a day since we met," he said, drawing in a deep breath. "I gave him the best I had under my roof. And how did the dog pay me back? He stole my gold and my horse and he shot my Kaffir boy, who had the animal in his keeping. A dark-hearted man is Ephraim Bull. He's mad for mischief wherever he goes."

Nothing more was said about the departed Ephraim Bull. John Blessington was not the man lightly to assume guilt in any fellow-creature without some evidence against him. There was nothing but suspicion to put the crime of firing the barn upon the shoulders of the old man who had come and departed so strangely.

Hans Karder was disappointed, and he showed it in a characteristic fashion. Whenever he was labouring under any form of emotion he flew to

his favourite means of support, the fiery schnapps
—at home he drew it from a bottle, abroad he
drank it from a flask—and he took a sip, as
he termed it, now. It would have been a
copious drink to an ordinary imbiber of strong
liquor.

The house of Barren Lands was larger than
that which had been destroyed on Golden Farm,
but it was not so carefully constructed. Nor were
there the interior comforts which had marked the
home of John Blessington. The one thing com-
mendable about it was its cleanliness, and the
credit of that was due to Hans Karder's *vrow*.

A Kaffir "boy" came out of the cattle-yard to
receive the orders of his master. He kept at a
safe distance, with his eyes on the Boer's right
hand, as if he had been accustomed to receive a
blow with the word of command.

"Wanga," said the Boer, "hitch the oxen into
the waggon."

The swarthy Kaffir "boy" crept away, and in
half an hour a team of eight oxen and waggon
appeared at the door. The men took their places
inside it and rode slowly back to Golden Farm,
the Boer smoking all the way, and occasionally
paying attention to his flask. He was in a silent,
thoughtful mood.

The loading up took time, and the afternoon

had arrived when the waggon started on its home journey with the Boer, Jan, and the women inside. John Blessington and his boys rode their horses, and drove their small herd of cows before them. It was arranged with Hans Karder that for awhile they were to be put out to graze on a small fertile bit of land near the kopje.

Jan had hardly exchanged a word with Sam and Joe ; and Polly, though the young Boer was disposed to be attentive to her, would have none of him. The Boer's *vrow* was a heavy-eyed, silent woman, more slave than wife at home, one of the class who are rarely permitted to sit at table with their lords and masters, victims of an old domestic law of Boer life. They wait upon the men and boys of the household, and eat alone when the males have appeased their appetites.

When the waggon arrived at the Boer's house, the oxen were taken out by Wanga, who was the recipient of an entirely uncalled-for brutal kick from Jan as he passed by.

As Sam was following Jan, the Kaffir moved aside in apprehension of a further illustration of the cruelty of the whites, but was startled by hearing a kind word addressed to him.

"You need not fear me," said Sam, in a low tone. "I am very sorry for you, my poor fellow."

D

He entered the house, leaving Wanga to reflect, with unbounded astonishment, on a red-letter episode in his life. He had been spoken to kindly by a white man. Hitherto Wanga's white world of humanity had been limited to the Boer kind.

Apparently the welcome of the Boer was a hearty one. Hans Karder took John Blessington round his place to show him the cattle, for he had a fair stock and they seemed to have been well fed. He bade his guests treat his house as their own, and laid aside his prejudice against eating with women in favour of Mrs. Blessington. His own wife, when curtly invited by him, refused to sit at table.

"As I have lived here to this day," she said, "so it shall be to the end."

Jan did not affect the amiable host with Sam and Joe. He took himself off in the evening, and left them to themselves. As they were working near the farmhouse, Wanga sidled up to Sam and touched him on the arm.

"Your house burn," he said, with his eyes starting out of his head. "Me know who make fire."

A sharp, angry utterance startled them all, and the boys, turning quickly, saw Hans Karder hard by, with a frown, dark as a thunder-cloud, upon his face.

CHAPTER VII.

THE DISAPPEARANCE OF WANGA.

NOTWITHSTANDING his dark looks, Hans Karder betrayed no anger in his speech as he addressed the shrinking Kaffir "boy." His suavity was quite a revelation to Sam and Joe, who had ever associated him with all that was coarse and unmannerly in his address.

"You shall tell us all about it by-and-by, Wanga," he said, "but you must not lie as you too often do—go and see to the horses."

The Kaffir stole away to the stables, and the Boer, lingering with the boys, talked of his servant as one "born to lie"—according to Hans Karder, the truth was not in him, and therefore could not come out of his mouth.

The brothers left the Boer and entered the house, where they found their father and mother earnestly discussing their prospects. The outlook was very bad indeed. The cutting of timber, bringing it in from a distance, and rebuilding the house and barns, would be the work of two months or more. There was no corn with which to make bread, and the little money John Blessington was possessed of he had stored away in a bank at Natal.

"I can't go away and leave you here," he sighed, "but some money I must have to get through the winter."

Hans Karder joined them and seemed to have an intuitive knowledge of the subject they were discussing. He filled his pipe and lighted it, then brought out his bottle of schnapps and mixed himself a stiff mug of spirit and water.

"Neighbours," he said, "I'm going to make you a last offer. I'll give you a hundred pounds and my house and farm for yours—and I'll be gone in a week. Ye needn't fear for my comfort. The Karders have trekked too often to mind living in camp. I've my waggon, and that's enough for me until the new house is built."

"I'll think it over," said John Blessington.

"Aye, neighbour, it's but wise of you to take time ere you shut down a bargain," remarked the Boer.

He emptied his mug of strong liquor, and was mixing another, when John Blessington laid a hand upon his arm.

"You take too much of that stuff, neighbour," he said; "it's no friend to you or any man."

"'YOU TAKE TOO MUCH OF THAT STUFF, NEIGHBOUR.'" (*p.* 52.)

Hans Karder knitted his brows and went on mixing his drink. "I've a bit of work to do to-night," he said, "and this stuff gives me the heart for anything."

There was no turning him from it, and the second potion was followed by a third. Drink did not make him hilarious, or even talkative, for he lapsed into sullen silence, and sat brooding in his chair, with a hard look upon his massive face.

Many of the household goods saved from the fire of Golden Farm were stored away in one of the outhouses of Barren Lands, and the door secured with a lock, of which John Blessington had the key. Though the country was, in a general sense, free from ordinary criminals, Hans Karder reminded his guest that the Kaffir was not to be trusted. That, at any rate, was his experience, he said.

"There are good and bad among them," said John Blessington, "just as we find among the whites. I fancy the Kaffir is much as we make him. He is, humanly speaking, composed of very pliable material."

Hans Karder would not have it so. He declared that the only means of instilling sound principles into the Kaffir was by the frequent application of the sjambok, and he doggedly stuck to his expressed belief.

"You must get at him through his skin," he said.

The shed used as a storehouse was not a marvellously strong structure. The roof especially was frail, thin planking, nailed together in a very unworkmanlike manner. Here and there a plank was loose, and Sam suggested he should make them secure.

Jan, who was prowling about hard by, heard him make the offer to Hans Karder, and he came forward to make an objection.

"I built the shed, or helped to do it," he said, "and I can look to any repairs that want doing."

"Then there 'll be a waiting for them to be done," said his father, grimly.

Jan sulkily said he wasn't quite such a skulker as he was thought to be, and forthwith got a ladder, hammer and nails, and mounted to the roof. Sam offered to assist him, and was told to go away.

"I want to be let alone," Jan snarled, and Sam good-humouredly left him to his task. In one of the stock-yards he came across Wanga, and recalled the Kaffir's having spoken of being in possession of some knowledge of how the fire happened at Golden Farm.

Sam stood and watched him tending some cattle for a time. It is an undeniable fact that veracity is not so much cultivated by the Kaffir as it ought to be, and the possibility of being told an untruth by Wanga deterred Sam from questioning him. Ephraim Bull was supposed to be the incendiary, and there was not a tittle of evidence against any other living person. But there was no absolute proof that the strange man who had come and gone during the harvest time had aught to do with the calamity, unless Hans Karder's word was to be taken. Sam hesitated to do that, but at the same time he desired to be just, even to a man he disliked. A Kaffir who hates his master does not stick at trifles when speaking to his detriment, and it was within the bounds of possibility Wanga might declare Hans Karder set fire to the barn, and there would be only his bare assertion to support an accusation.

" Better let it go for the present," thought Sam, as he turned away; and being in a musing mood, he wandered unconsciously back to the outhouse where he had left Jan repairing the roof.

The ladder was there, and the hammer and nails lay upon the roof, but Jan was not in sight. One of the planks of the roof had been removed, leaving a long and widish gap. As Sam stood there wonderingly, the victim of a surprise, he heard sounds of somebody moving about inside the outhouse, and apparently shifting some of the articles stored therein.

Surely Jan had not fallen so low as to develop into a common thief? At all events, Sam had a right to ask what he was doing inside the out-house, and he nimbly ascended by the ladder to the roof. Lying down, he peered through the opening made by the removal of the plank, and saw Jan busy searching among the things belonging to Sam and his friends.

"What are you doing there?" he demanded.

Jan looked up, and a hot flush spread over his face. It passed away, leaving his cheeks sallow.

"What do you think I am doing?" he asked huskily.

"Can't say," answered Sam, laconically; "you had better leave things alone for a bit. We can arrange them ourselves better, by-and-by."

Sam moved away a little from the opening, and turning half round saw Hans Karder and Wanga below. The Kaffir stood a little way behind his master with a grin upon his face.

"What's the matter there?" asked Karder.

"Jan's rummaging among our goods," replied Sam, "and it's a thing he ought not to do."

Jan's head appeared through the opening in the roof, and his sullen eyes were bent upon the upturned face of his father. The old Boer was especially angry with him for being so indiscreet as to allow himself to be found in the act of performing a shabby trick upon a guest.

"Come down, Jan," he said, "and let Sam Blessington finish the roof. What were you doing in there?"

"Looking for something of my own," replied Jan, curtly; "my sjambok, if you wish to know all the particulars."

"The one you told me you had lost?" asked Hans Karder. Jan nodded, and glanced viciously at Sam. The old Boer read that glance, and understood what had happened.

"Come down, Jan," he said harshly; "it's a lie you've told me, and I'll not forgive you. Come down."

"If you lay a hand on me I'll blurt out things," said Jan. Hans Karder turned on his heel and walked quickly away.

Wanga's face was now broad and shiny with mirth, and Jan, who was sliding down the ladder, face outwards, and holding on by his arms and legs, as boys are fond of doing at the risk of a fall, asked him what he was grinning at?

"'Bout dat Golden Farm fire," replied Wanga, promptly; "dat all queer—so—*we* know."

Having thus expressed himself, in a vague but suggestive fashion, Wanga hurried away to some duty he had to perform in another part of the farm. Jan looked up at Sam, who was arranging the plank over the hole of the roof, prior to nailing it down, and their eyes met.

"I suppose you have been putting Wanga up to telling lies against us?" said Jan.

"You know better than that," replied Sam; "any way, Wanga is not responsible for your rummaging among our goods."

"I only wanted to find the sjambok you stole from me," growled Jan.

"Stole from you?"

"Yes, what else do you call it?" demanded Jan. "You can't say I gave it to you."

"I'll give it back to you at a more fitting time," said Sam, looking steadily at Jan, "and I'll ask you to go away, for I'm in no humour to be charged with theft."

Jan did not like the look on Sam's face, and he prudently retired. Sam eased off his anger by driving the nails well home, and soon completed his job of repairing the roof. He left it sounder than it had been for a year or more in the past.

Sam and Joe, when in their own room, invariably had a little talk ere they went to sleep. Wanga was uppermost in their minds that night, so they talked of him and wondered if he really had anything of importance to tell.

"I can't feel at home here, with the Karders," said Sam, passionately, "and I am sorry we ever came. Just remember what happened before harvest, Joe. It may be wrong to think evil of anyone, but I can't help believing that Jan was wicked enough to try to bury us alive. And there's Hans Karder—I am certain he could tell us who fired our barn."

"You don't know," murmured Joe; "you only think so. Remember what father always insists on: Don't believe ill of anyone until you are sure he deserves it."

They undressed and got into bed. In a few moments both were sound asleep.

A wild, despairing cry awoke the stillness of the night. Sam started up in his bed, but Joe slept on. "Was it a dream?" the awakened boy asked himself.

The cry was not repeated. There was no sound within or without the house for awhile, and Sam lay down to sleep again.

Hark! what is that? A footstep outside surely, as of one stealing up to the house. Sam slipped out of bed and glided to the window. It was a moonlight night, and coming towards the house, with slow, unsteady steps, was Hans Karder with a heavy stick in his hand.

Pulling up half-way, he glared about him with

the rays of the moon lighting up his face. It was distorted with passion, and Sam shuddered as he gazed upon the man.

Whatever he was looking for, he failed to find it, and came on to the house. The snap of the door closing, and his heavy footsteps in the passage below, followed. Sam crept into bed again, and after a restless hour or so, lost all knowledge of things good and bad in sleep.

The morning came, and the voice of Hans Karder in the stock-yard, roaring like an angry bull, aroused the boys. They hastily dressed and went down to learn the cause of the Boer's excitement. He was still raging about and calling for Wanga, who had disappeared from the farm in the night.

Jan appeared and was ordered to saddle his father's horse. While this was being done, the elder Boer ate a crust of bread, drank enough spirit and water to set his blood on fire, and presently, with his gun slung at his back, rode away.

"If he comes across Wanga," grinned Jan, "he'll shoot him on sight; that's how we treat runaway Kaffir boys."

"It would be murder," said Sam, hotly.

"Poof!" rejoined Jan, contemptuously; "it's no murder to shoot a Kaffir. I'd do it and think nothing of it."

There was one kind, good Karder in the house, the sad-eyed *vrow* of the Boer. She said little, but she did much for Mrs. Blessington and Polly.

They responded heartily, and gave back to the woman for her kindness what she had ever lacked from husband and son—grateful thanks.

The day passed and the Boer did not return. Jan expressed no anxiety, and the *vrow*, whatever may have been in her heart, made no sign. The night came and he was still away, and so on to another day.

"Something has happened to him," said John Blessington. "Jan, you must go in search of your father."

"No, indeed," replied Jan, curtly, "I've something better to do."

"Then I will go," said John Blessington. And having saddled his horse, he departed on his errand to help the man, his false friend, who at that very hour was lying in the kopje with an assegai thrust into his side.

CHAPTER VIII.

THE EXCHANGE OF THE FARMS.

In the open country a horseman could be easily espied at a distance, and John Blessington furthermore guessed that the Kaffir must have taken refuge near the kopje, and there Hans Karder would seek him. So to the kopje the Englishman went, and there he speedily came upon the man he sought.

He was lying on his back, with one of the short spears, known as assegais, buried in his side. Hard by was his horse, peacefully feeding on the scant herbage around. John Blessington hurriedly dismounted and tenderly raised the head of the Boer, who was breathing fitfully.

The first thing to be done was to extract the keen weapon and bind up the wound. Skilled in a crude way in such matters, John Blessington soon performed the needed amateur surgery, and as he completed it, Hans Karder opened his eyes.

"I was taken in ambush," he muttered, "but I

dropped him. You'll find Wanga over by that rock yonder. Old Hans Karder never misses his aim. Give me a drink from my flask, neighbour."

"Better have some water. The spirit is bad for you—it will throw you into a fever."

"Water is for women. Strong drink is for men."

"For madmen," muttered John Blessington.

But the Boer could have no strong drink then. On his pockets being examined it was found that his flask was missing. The rifle and cartridge belt of Hans Karder were also gone. The Boer shook with rage as he tottered towards a spring of water, assisted by the Englishman.

"I missed him," he kept muttering. "Hans Karder missed! Look over yonder and make sure. It don't seem natural that I should shoot and waste my powder and lead."

John Blessington crossed over to the spot pointed out by the Boer. Behind a boulder that was about breast high of a man there was a dark stain upon the ground, but nothing more. Hans Karder might have failed to kill, but his aim had not been wholly ineffective.

"I beat him last night, as he meant to tell lies," said the Boer, "and having got me down, why did he leave the breath of life in me? It was not like Kaffir work."

E

John Blessington could offer no suggestion on the matter. He thought it possible that Wanga was possessed of a more merciful nature than his master, but he did not say so. That line of reasoning would have been wasted on Hans Karder.

By riding at walking pace, and with the Englishman by his side supporting him, the Boer succeeded in getting home. He was assisted to bed by his *vrow*, who exhibited no grief, nor any emotion whatever.

The wound of Hans Karder was not in itself dangerous, but if he maintained his drinking habits the worst was to be anticipated. Jan was urged by all not to keep his father supplied with liquor. He merely grinned in reply.

" Ye're a lot of babies," he said to Sam three days later, "and can drink nothing but milk. It doesn't warm the blood and make you feel as if you could throw the strongest man on earth."

" That's the falsity of drink," returned Sam; "it makes you feel as if you could do this and that, but you can't. You drink the poisonous stuff and it's horrible in a boy. I don't want to boast, but though you are older and taller than I am, you are not so strong."

" I'll try ye at that," said Jan, viciously.

They went into the barn and wrestled there.

Jan did all he knew, and exerted himself until the veins stood out on his forehead, but he failed to throw Sam, who quietly waited until his big antagonist was exhausted, and then with no visibly great effort threw him down upon a heap of straw.

"Milk and water wins the day," he said, and laughing merrily, walked away.

Jan muttered something about "being too much of a man to be teetotal," and sauntered off in the opposite direction.

There were grave whisperings about the house in relation to Hans Karder. After the first day he refused to see anyone but Jan, who took his father's illness lightly. He was not only free from sorrow, but frequently burst into fits of laughter when remonstrated with for supplying the wounded man with drink, as it seemed, both day and night.

On the night of the fifth day of Hans Karder's being in his room, Jan suddenly appeared before John Blessington and his family, who were having supper with the *vrow*.

"Father wants you," said Jan, curtly.

John Blessington, whom he addressed, rose with a fear in his heart and went out with the boy, who walked down the passage quickly and threw open the bedroom door.

"He's dying," said Jan, "and he wants you to do something to comfort him."

There was only a small light burning, so that the room was in semi-darkness. Hans Karder on his couch, shaded by heavy curtains, could be but dimly seen.

"Sit down, neighbour," he moaned, in a voice so low that he was scarcely heard; "it's about the change of farms that I wish to see you."

"I thought it might have been something more important to you—the welfare of your immortal soul. It is all-important to you that you should be at peace with God," replied John Blessington.

"Sign agreement for the exchange," moaned Hans Karder, "for my lifetime—no more. It will comfort and help me to know I held the Golden Farm for an hour, as I set my heart on it. I'll talk to ye of better things after."

John Blessington did not refuse him, but it cost him a struggle. The man was dying; and having his mind at ease about this worldly matter, might he not think of higher things? Paper and pen and ink were ready, and in brief terms the agreement to exchange farms for the Boer's lifetime, he paying the sum of fifty pounds in cash, was drawn up and signed. Jan was the witness.

"Now, neighbour," said John Blessington,

turning to Hans Karder, "that is done with, and—— "

"I'll talk to you no more to-night," said the Boer, with a sudden change of voice. "Neighbour, I've taken your word that the drink was bad for me, *and touched none of it as I lay here.* Me and Jan have been shamming. The Golden Farm is *mine*—mine, and you must take to Barren Lands, whether ye will or no."

CHAPTER IX.

OPEN ENMITY.

IT was a shock to John Blessington to find he had been so grossly imposed upon, but it was more than that to him to learn that a man could be so debased as to feign being on the verge of death to gain a worldly end. He sat dumb and still, overwhelmed by the repulsion he felt towards Hans Karder.

The Boer sat up in his bed, a bare-faced, hypocritical impostor, and was not ashamed. Jan, a worthy son of his father, rubbed his hands and chuckled with delight. At length John Blessington found his tongue.

"Hans Karder," he said, slowly, "you are a scoundrel, and although I have been cheated into making a bad bargain with you, I'll put up with it."

"You've got to," replied the Boer, with heavy facetiousness; "an Englishman can't repudiate an agreement made with a Boer in this country."

70

"I have been easy-going and simple, perhaps, Hans Karder," said John Blessington, "but I would not change places with you for ten Golden Farms. Sin prospers for awhile in the night-time, but sorrow and shame come in the morning."

He rose and walked from the room, closing the door quietly. There was none of the passion in his words or actions that might have been shown by an angered and outraged man. There was not a wrinkle of wrath upon his face as he entered the room where his family and the *vrow* had assembled.

"Come out, my people, from under this treacherous roof," he said, "until it is purged of the presence of a cunning scoundrel."

In a few brief words he told them how he had been befooled. His wife listened with a white face, and his children with dismay upon their countenances.

"You were always too trustful, John," said Mrs. Blessington ; " too simple of heart, too kindly, perhaps."

"Repudiate the contract," said Sam, hotly.

"My boy," replied his father, "it would only lead to our losing all and being driven like vagabonds out of the land. No; I'll take the Barren Lands and trust in our Heavenly Guide to put right the wrong I suffer from."

The Blessingtons left the house, taking with them only a few necessaries, and camped in the open air. The boys gathered some wood and made a fire, by which they sat with their father watching, until the day returned. They would trust the Boer no more, believing he might be bad enough to murder them as they slept. The mother and daughter, well wrapped in blankets, alone sought repose.

The exulting Boer was up early in the morning, and aided by Jan, got out the waggon and proceeded to fill it with his household goods. The *vrow* helped them, as a slave might have done, and by noon all the possessions of the house were packed for removal. The Blessingtons remained by their camp fire and held aloof from all communion with the man.

Jan gathered the cattle together and let loose two dogs, trained to keep them in a drove. Then the Boer came down to the little camp fire, with a small bag in his grasp.

" This is the promised gold, neighbour," he said. " I may deal as a sharp man, but I am honest."

" Put the money on the ground; it is my right," replied John Blessington ; " and go your way."

" I'll drink to you before I go," said the Boer, derisively, as he produced a bottle and put it to his lips. " I've missed my good schnapps sorely."

"You have in it a greater enemy than I shall ever be to you," answered John Blessington.

The Boer laughed and turned upon his heel.

His *vrow* was in the waggon, and Jan was holding the horses ready to start. After a short delay the Boer and his belongings moved away towards Golden Farm. Then John Blessington led his family up to their new home.

"It will be many, many days," said Mrs. Blessington, "ere I can abide in peace under this roof."

Jan, in an hour or so, came galloping back, and reined up by the door. Sam was near the cattle-yard, filling a trough with water.

"Hey, there!" shouted Jan.

"What do you want?" demanded Sam.

"Father says if you allow your cattle to stray on Golden Farm, he will treat 'em as if they were gemsbok," cried Jan hilariously.

"And if you stay here another minute," retorted Sam, "I'll give you a sound thrashing."

"Are we to be open enemies?" demanded Jan, bending low in the saddle, and peering viciously in Sam's face.

"If we are, you cannot complain," replied Sam, "having so long been our enemy in secret. Keep away from us and you have nothing to fear."

"I am not afraid," said Jan, snapping his fingers;

"it is you who may have cause to shake in your boots. We want no English here!"

He gave his horse a smart cut with the whip and galloped away, leaving Sam boiling over with the impetuous anger of youth. Polly, who had been watching them from the window of the dairy, came out and put her arms about her brother's neck.

"Come in, Sam!" she said. "At least we have no Karder to darken the house to-night."

Yes, the house was free of the Karders, but it was not as if they were free of them for ever and back in their old home. Neither Joe nor Sam were able to avoid a feeling of bitterness as they thought of Jan triumphantly living on the apparently better farm, and chuckling over the astuteness of his father, who had brought about the exchange by cunning and falsehood.

Joe sat on a big stone by the door, with his elbows on his knees and his chin resting in his hands. It was thus Sam found him after he had stabled his horse and was returning to the house.

"There's work to do, Joe," he said; "the things we stored must be got out and cleaned before they can be put into the rooms."

"That Jan is a cur," said Joe.

"Granted; and a cur is not worth worrying

about," returned Sam. "As I told you before, he is to be left to me."

The task of emptying the outhouse was soon performed, for their household goods were few. The boys set to work cleaning them, and by-and-by Polly came out to help, while her mother prepared dinner. From an old chest of drawers, Sam brought out a sjambok, which he laid aside. Joe recognised it as the one taken from Jan.

"I have wondered what became of that thing," he said.

"I put it away," replied Sam, "and had almost forgotten all about it when Jan, by something he did, reminded me of it the other day. I intend to give it back to him at an early opportunity."

"I wouldn't do it," said Joe.

"I have made up my mind to do it," said Sam, "and we'll talk no more about it, please."

Joe did not pursue the subject, and the work of making the home orderly and habitable occupied the whole of the afternoon. In the evening Sam rode out alone, taking Jan's sjambok with him in his hand, and with his own strung to the saddle, in the orthodox fashion. Joe watched him go, and asked no questions. It was dark when he returned, and he still had the two sjamboks in his possession.

John Blessington had good cause 'to be downcast, but he showed no signs of being in a depressed condition of mind. The worst was known, he verily believed, of his enemy·; he had done his worst, and the less said about the past the better. His talk was of the future operations on the farm, which he believed he could improve in many ways and make it more profitable than Hans Karder had ever attempted to do.

They retired early, in conformity with the habit of their lives. Joe and Sam were too tired to talk much, and the former slept without a dream, as far as he was aware of. When he awoke the day was an hour old and Sam was up and gone.

Joe lost no time in getting through his simple morning toilet and hastening below. Mrs. Blessington and Polly had already got through a considerable portion of their early morning duties; and when Joe expostulated with them for letting him sleep so long, they told him it was Sam's wish he should not be disturbed.

"He helped father to get through the milking before sunrise," said Polly, "and then went for a ride. Father is gone to see if he can shoot a bird or two for dinner."

"Which way did Sam go?" asked Joe.

Polly fancied he rode in the direction of

Golden Farm, but would not be sure of it. She noticed he had two sjamboks with him, and wondered why one should not be considered by him to be enough.

"We have very few cattle to round up," she remarked, "and I have not heard of any of them straying."

"He had a reason for taking two sjamboks," said Joe. "Sam never does anything without its being good or necessary. I'll have a ride round on the chance of coming across him."

Joe saddled his stout pony and rode away in the direction of Golden Farm. For the greater part the land was open, and but here and there a kopje, or a clump of trees, broke up the view of the horizon. Riding round one of the former, Joe came upon a scene that was very startling to him. It was Jan riding towards him at a furious pace with Sam in hot pursuit.

Sam was whirling the lash of a sjambok over his head, more as one does it for pleasure than with a vicious intent, and his face was lighted up with laughter. That of Jan, on the contrary, was dark with terror, and gasping appeals for mercy broke from his lips.

He rode with a loose rein, and as the ground was rough in places, it was no marvel that his horse stumbled and fell, throwing him heavily.

He fell to the ground with a thud, rolling
over twice ere he came to rest upon his back,
and staring in a bewildered manner at the sky.
Joe and Sam arrived beside him together, and
reined up near the fallen and deeply humiliated
Jan.

He relieved their momentary anxiety about
the possibility of his having broken some of
his bones by sitting up, rubbing his head rue-
fully, and then slowly rising to his feet. His
horse had picked itself up and was galloping back
in the direction of its stable at Golden Farm.

Sam leapt down, sjambok in hand, and drew
the lash slowly and painlessly across the back
of Jan.

"Consider you have been whipped," said Sam,
"and now you can have your sjambok back
again."

He cut the lash in two, broke the handle
and tossed the pieces at the feet of Jan, who
stared heavily at him, breathing hard from the
effects of his fall. It had shaken him up somewhat, and deprived him of his full breathing
powers for a time. He felt the indignity of
having his sjambok given to him in pieces more
than he would have smarted under the sting of
its lash.

"You will get something more than a sjamboking," he said slowly; "we are going to drive every rooinek out of the country."

"The rooineks will return," said Sam; "you people are making a rod for your own backs. Why should we be enemies? It is not the desire of the English."

"I'm your enemy for good and all," said Jan, as he spurned away the pieces of his sjambok with his feet; "you wait a bit and see what will be done."

"We are not afraid of you," said Sam, contemptuously; "don't forget. You are to consider yourself thrashed. Good-day."

"I am glad I left him to you," said Joe, as the brothers rode back to Barren Lands; "you settled the sjambok business in first-rate style. It was better than giving him a beating."

"I was sorely tempted to do it," said Sam, laughing, "but when he turned tail on seeing me—I was waiting for him behind a boulder near a kopje—I decided to be content with scaring him. His fall gave me the opportunity to add the giving of his sjambok back to him in pieces."

Polly observed that Sam had but one sjambok when he came home, and asked sundry questions concerning it. Joe told her the story of it throughout.

"That is just like Sam," said Polly; "he always does what is right."

CHAPTER X.

THE TRIUMPH OF HANS KARDER.

IN any other country such a transaction as that which deprived John Blessington of the Golden Farm would have been almost impossible. But being in one of the loneliest parts of the Transvaal, with none of his countrymen near to support him, he was entirely at the mercy of the wily Boer, Hans Karder.

There were other Boers in the Jugersdorf district, but they lived on scattered farms at a distance. Very rarely indeed had John Blessington seen one of them. Occasionally he had noticed them come on their horses to Barren Lands, and after a brief stay, ride away without favouring him with a friendly call.

He did not grieve over their neglect, for there was no affinity between him and them. They were burly and rough in their ways, and fond of the drink that he abhorred.

A few days after the exchange of land, the

outlying Boers came riding in and wended their way to Golden Farm. Some secret understanding must have existed between them and Hans Karder, for they came provided with sundry tools, strung upon the pommels of their saddles, or strapped to their backs, wherewith to assist their triumphant countryman in the erection of a new farm-house and outbuildings.

Some came out of their road to Barren Lands house, ostensibly to ask for a drink of milk or water, but really with the object of conveying to the Blessingtons their sense of being of a superior race. They would ride up to the door and call for what they wanted, as if they were ill-bred customers at a wayside hostelry. The boys, with the impetuosity of their years, would have resented it and refused to give anything to their uncouth visitors, but John Blessington restrained them.

There were times, however, when he found it hard to endure the insolence of the callers. On one occasion, especially, matters bordered on a quarrel that might have ended with fatal results. A Boer and his son, the very counterpart of Hans Karder and Jan, rode up to the farm and espied John Blessington in the cattle-yard, busy mending a drinking-trough. As was now the custom, Mrs. Blessington and the family had retired to one of the back rooms of the house and shut

F

themselves in, Sam and Joe fuming with indignation.

"Hi!—you Englishmen," shouted the elder Boer, "we want drink."

"Bide a bit," calmly replied John Blessington. "I've a nail or two to put in here, and then the job's done."

"A Boer doesn't wait," was the rejoinder, with an imperative motion of the hand. "Give us what we want at once."

"If you can't wait a minute or so," said John Blessington in his even way, "ride on to the next farm."

"We'll go in and help ourselves," growled the Boer, defiantly.

He turned his horse and moved towards the door of the house, with his grinning son following him. John Blessington, retaining the hammer he was using, took a short cut across the cattle-yard, leapt over the wooden fence with the lightness of a much younger man, and at the entrance to his house barred the way of the Boers.

"Keep your saddles," he said determinedly, "and say what you will have, water or milk?"

"Neither," answered the Boer; "have you no whisky or schnapps?"

"No; we touch nothing in that way here," said John Blessington.

"I'll have some milk," said the younger Boer winking at his father.

The Englishman fetched a mug of milk and handed it to the boy, who flung the liquid over John Blessington and took refuge behind his father, who had drawn a revolver from his belt and held it ready for use.

"Go your way," said the outraged man; "it was a boy who did that, or I should not bear it so calmly."

"Fetch another mug of the baby stuff for *me*," said the Boer, "and I'll serve you the same way."

John Blessington walked into the house with a steady step and entered the dairy. As he was dipping the mug into a pan of milk, his wife and children, who had heard what passed, emerged from their retreat. The boys were flushed and hot with indignation, the mother and daughter white with apprehension. "Let me take the milk to him," urged Mrs. Blessington.

"You needn't fear," answered her husband; "there is no fight in the coward."

He took down his rifle, and with it in one hand and the mug of milk in the other he went to the door. The two Boers espied him coming down the passage carrying his rifle, and rode away with a promptitude that excited roars of laughter from Sam and Joe.

" What did I tell you ? " said John Blessington, grimly ; " the Boer is a fighter from behind rocks and trees. Hang up my gun, Sam ; it won't be wanted yet."

And so it proved, for no more Boers came to exercise their gift of insolence on the lone family. The work on Golden Farm proceeded rapidly, and within a month the house and barns were completed. The event was celebrated by the assemblage of a score or more of Boers, who spent the day in drinking, feasting, and firing triumphant salvos with their rifles.

John Blessington was in an anxious state of mind all that day. He knew the Boer nature and feared they might finish their orgie by paying him an unwelcome visit; and this fear was justified, for as he stood by the door soon after nightfall, the heavy thud of feet of approaching horses fell upon his ears.

CHAPTER XI.

FRIENDS OUT OF THE DARKNESS.

THE position was one of peril. It sometimes—nay, too often—happens that men who are kindly disposed in their habits when sober will become dangerous under the influence of drink. What might not the rough Boers, after their day of excessive indulgence in strong liquor, be prepared to do?

Barren Lands was a lonely spot, and a dark deed done there would perhaps never be heard of by the outside world. The Boers hated the Englishman, and were too ready in the use of arms when it served them. The whole of the Blessington family could be made away with, and their poor farm turned to waste, without a whisper of it reaching more civilised places.

"I may have to use arms in defence of my home. It's sorrowful work, but I am not the aggressor," muttered John Blessington, as he stepped in and closed the door. The only fasten-

85

ing, beyond the ordinary latch, was a heavy wooden bar made to rest in two iron sockets. He put it in its place and passed on to the room where his wife and family had gathered together.

"The Boers are coming," he said; "and with the drink in them, there is no knowing what they may be ready to do."

"Oh, the baseness and cruelty of it all!" sobbed his wife, suddenly breaking down.

"They may stop at annoying us," rejoined John Blessington; "perhaps they may content themselves with riding round the house, yelling and firing their weapons. We shall see."

Polly, who had hitherto restrained her tears, burst out crying now, and for a few minutes there was a scene of distressful emotion. But delay was dangerous, and having spoken a few comforting words, the farmer bade his boys follow him.

There was an unglazed window overlooking the land in front of the house. It had a plain wooden shutter that was taken down by day. He removed it now, and took his stand by the opening with his boys behind him. They were prepared for any emergency, and were determined to defend their home against all comers.

Sweeping up like the wind of a tornado came

"THEY WERE DETERMINED TO DEFEND THEIR HOME." (*p.* 86.)

the Boers, some roaring a drinking song, others yelling out senseless threats against all who had British blood in their veins. A word of command was given, and the voice of Hans Karder was recognised by the father and sons. The Boers dismounted, and for a minute or two were engaged in tethering their horses together. Then in a body they advanced to the house, suddenly giving up their song and shouts and lapsing into grim silence.

"Come further at your peril!" cried John Blessington.

The Boers stopped short, and there was some rapid whispering among them. Then Hans Karder stood out, dimly seen in the starlight, and in assumed friendly tones addressed the Englishman.

"Neighbour Blessington," he said, "this is a sorry welcome to friends, who come to say farewell to you ere they depart for their homes."

"They are no friends of mine," answered John Blessington; "let them go their way and leave me and mine in peace."

"Not until they have drunk with you," cried Hans Karder, "though it be in nothing better than the milk and water you give your guests."

"None of you shall enter here to-night," said John Blessington, firmly. "Stand back!"

A shot was fired from the midst of the Boers, and the bullet whistled through the open window, passing just over the head of Sam, and splintering the wooden wall of the room behind him.

It would have been nothing short of cowardice or folly to have reasoned with such men any longer, and a moment later Hans Karder fell, disabled, but not seriously hurt.

His friends scuttled back, with fierce cries bursting from their lips. They took refuge behind their horses, and from that point of vantage rested their rifles on the saddles and poured in a volley directed at the open window of the farmhouse.

But John Blessington, though as brave a man as ever lived, was wary, and a whispered word from him to his sons as the Boers were retreating directed them to throw themselves upon the floor. As they lay there the storm of leaden missiles went harmlessly over their prostrate forms, doing no harm beyond splitting and perforating the wooden planks of which the room was built.

"Spare your fire," said John Blessington to his boys as they were rising, hot and eager to return the shots of the Boers; "you can only injure the horses, and they are not responsible for this night's work."

Suddenly there was a lull, and a Boer called

out in thunderous tones for the Englishman to give himself up to them.

His answer was: "Never with life."

The firing was renewed, and the din increased. The wooden walls of the building were broken in fifty places, the interior was a scene of wreckage. But there was no sign of yielding from the inmates, not even a sob or a cry from the mother and daughter, who had adopted the tactics of the father and sons, and were lying prone upon the floor of their place of refuge.

There were prayers to God for help on the lips of all, when from out of the darkness of the plain some mounted men swept up, and the chaotic sounds of men engaged in a desperate encounter echoed far and wide.

CHAPTER XII.

THE REAL GOLDEN FARM.

WHAT did it mean? John Blessington and his boys sprang to their feet and looked eagerly from the window. Outside there was a misty mass of struggling men, mounted and on foot, that speedily broke up until only those on horseback remained.

"Bolted for their lives," said a voice cheerily, "as they always do in open fight. What fiends'- work were they doing here?"

Then in louder tones the speaker cried, "John Blessington, we are friends. Open the door and let us in."

The Englishman hastened to comply with this request, and pulling out the wooden bar, he threw back the door. About a dozen mounted men were outside, and half their number dismounted and came in.

"Get a light, friend Blessington," said the foremost; "you have no further cause to fear the Boers."

Mrs Blessington had heard what passed, and now appeared with a lighted lamp in her hand. The glare of it revealed two familiar faces— those of Ephraim Bull and Wanga the Kaffir. The others had the appearance of well-to-do men of the type seen in Natal.

It was a surprise, indeed, to have such good company there, but the explanation of their coming had to be deferred for a little while. John Blessington remembered Hans Karder, and his first thought was to have his hurt seen to. "Enemy as he has been," he said, "I'll not leave him like a wounded weasel to die uncared for."

Hans Karder was brought into the house in an exhausted condition. They took him to John Blessington's own room, and laid him on the bed, whereupon Ephraim Bull, experienced in such matters, examined him and briefly reported: "No bones broken; he is not badly hurt, and is only exhausted a bit."

The story of Ephraim Bull and his reappearance was very simple. He was a prospector, and wandering in the Jugersdorp region, he had discovered indications of gold there. They were pieces of quartz he was examining in his bedroom the first night he stayed at Golden Farm, and he remained there for a time secretly to observe the peculiarities of the country.

Assured at last there was gold in the district, he went his way, but to make doubly sure, lingered for a day or two in the kopje. While he was there, Wanga fled from his brutal master, who had wounded him. Ephraim Bull, hearing the report of the rifle, **hurried** to the spot, and found the Kaffir lying on the ground senseless from the effect of the bullet. The prospector had no desire to reveal his presence there, but he felt kindly towards Wanga, and carried him to a place of safety. Together they eventually went to Natal.

There Ephraim Bull looked up certain speculators, to whom he gave his report, and a party was formed to come out and obtain possession of the gold-bearing district. And then came the final element of surprise in the story.

"It is here where the gold is to be found," Ephraim Bull said, "on Barren Lands, the true Golden Farm. I heard of your having been swindled into making an exchange with Karder from a Boer in Natal, who was chuckling over it. Be thankful, Mr. Blessington, for that exchange. You are now a rich man."

And so it proved. When the prospectors examined the hitherto seemingly valueless land they promptly offered John Blessington to take it off his hands for the sum of twenty thousand pounds. It is needless to say he closed at once with the offer, for he longed to return to the old country.

Next day Jan and his mother came over to Barren Lands, the *vrow* to see her wounded husband, and Jan, shamefaced and discomfited, to ask for forgiveness. He was more than surprised to find himself treated with quiet kindness, and remained in a thoughtful mood until he went away, taking his injured father in the waggon with him. The probability is he had at last learnt to profit by the noble example of forbearance shown by those whom he had persecuted.

Thus things turned about and light came out of the darkness. Barren Lands was the true Golden Farm, and the shock of the discovery may have had something to do with the early demise of Hans Karder. He lived just long enough to see the place he once despised develop into one of the richest gold mines in the country. Jan left the district and has not been heard of since.

But prior to this the Blessington family returned home, and the money they brought with them provided handsomely for the elders to live at ease and set the boys up in business. Instinct and associations led them to become farmers, and, despite the difficulties of cultivating our home lands, they prosper. Polly married one of their country friends, and became a model housewife.

Two things in relation to the past were never closely inquired into—the attempt to shoot John Blessington and the firing of his barn. There was little doubt about Hans Karder being guilty of both dark deeds, but John Blessington, when the subject was broached, would say, " What does it matter now? He was a foolish man, working against his own good. Let it all go."

So these things were buried, forgiven, if not forgotten, by the good man and his family.

THE END

PRINTED BY NEILL AND CO., LTD., EDINBURGH.

Following Jesus: A Bible Picture Book for the Young. Size 13½ × 10 inches. Contains 12 large and beautifully coloured Old and New Testament Scenes, with appropriate letterpress by D. J. D., Author of "Bible Pictures and Stories," etc. Handsome coloured cover, paper boards with cloth back 2s. 6d.

A charming gift-book for young children.

Brought to Jesus: A Bible Picture Book for Little Readers. Containing Twelve large New Testament Scenes, printed in colours, with appropriate letterpress by Mrs. G. E. Morton. Size, 13½ by 10 inches. Handsome coloured boards with cloth back. 2s. 6d.

Light for Little Footsteps; or, Bible Stories Illustrated. By the Author of "A Ride to Picture Land," etc. Size, 13½ by 10 inches. With beautiful coloured Cover and Frontispiece. Full of Pictures. 2s. 6d.

A Trip to Many Lands. By W. J. Forster, Author of "Uncle Zeph and his Yarns," etc. With Twenty-six Full-page Pictures. 4to. Cloth gilt. 2s. 6d.

Bible Pictures and Stories. Old and New Testament. In one Volume. Bound in handsome cloth covers, with Eighty-nine Full-page Illustrations by Eminent Artists. 2s. 6d.

Story of Jesus. For Little Children. By Mrs. G. E. Morton, Author of "Brought to Jesus," etc. Many Illustrations. Imperial 16mo. Cloth boards. 2s. 6d.

From " Castleton's ' Prep.' "

Victoria: Her Life and Reign. By Alfred E. Knight. New Edition. Large Crown 8vo. 320 pages. Cloth extra, 2s. 6d.; fancy cloth, gilt edges, 3s. 6d.

Castleton's "Prep." By Charlotte Murray, Author of "Through Grey to Gold," etc. Illustrated. Crown 8vo. Cloth boards, 2s. 6d.

Through Grey to Gold. By Charlotte Murray, Author of "Muriel Malone," etc. Illustrated. Crown 8vo. Cloth boards, 2s. 6d.

Muriel Malone; or From Door to Door. By Charlotte Murray Author of "Wardlaugh," etc. Illustrated. Crown 8vo. Cloth boards, 2s. 6d.

The success of the Author's story. "Wardlaugh," has led to these helpful Christian books being published. The character-sketching is good, and the interest well maintained from start to finish.

THE "RED MOUNTAIN" SERIES.

Crown 8vo. 320 pages. Illustrated. Handsomely bound in cloth. 2s. 6d. each.

Ice Bound; or, The Anticosti Crusoes. By Edward Roper, F.R.G.S., Author of "By Track and Trail through Canada." Eight Illustrations. Crown 8vo. Cloth boards, 2s. 6d.

The adventures, perils, and experiences of some shipwrecked persons on this ice-bound island are graphically described, the book affording capital reading and much information on the natural and physical conditions of life in this northern region.

On Winding Waters: A Tale of Adventure and Peril. By William Murray Graydon, Author of "The Fighting Lads of Devon," etc. Fully illustrated. Crown 8vo. Cloth boards, 2s. 6d.

A summer canoeing trip on a North American creek; describing, in the form of an exciting tale, the mishaps, perils and adventures of a party of students who spent their holiday on winding waters.

From "Ice Bound."

Burtons of Burdale (The). By John W. Kneeshaw, Author of "Norcliffe Court," etc. Illustrated. Crown 8vo.

Grand Chaco (The): A Boy's Adventures in an unknown Land. By G. Manville Fenn.

"Mr. Fenn has lost none of his imaginative power, and the boating adventures of his boy heroes in South America leave nothing to be desired."—*Athenæum.*

First in the Field: A Story of New South Wales. By G. Manville Fenn.

Loyal: A Story of the Mercantile Marine. By Arthur Collard. Illustrated.

Two Henriettas (The). By Emma Marshall, Author of "Eaglehurst Towers," etc.

Adventures of Don Lavington (The). By G. Manville Fenn. Illustrated. Large Crown 8vo. Cloth extra.

Crystal Hunters (The): A Boy's Adventures in the Higher Alps. By G. Manville Fenn. Illustrated. Large Crown 8vo. Cloth extra.

Norcliffe Court. By John W. Kneeshaw, Author of "A Black Shadow," "From Dusk to Dawn," etc.

By Sea-Shore, Wood, and Moorland: Peeps at Nature. By Edward Step, Author of "Plant Life," etc.

Eagle Cliff (The): A Tale of the Western Isles. By R. M. Ballantyne, Author of "Fighting the Flames," etc.

Edwin, The Boy Outlaw; or, The Dawn of Freedom in England. A Story of the Days of Robin Hood. By J. Frederic Hodgetts, Author of " Older England " etc.

England's Navy: Stories of its Ships and its Services With a Glance at some Navies of the Ancient World. By F. M Holmes, Author of " Great Works by Great Men," etc.

Green Mountain Boys (The): A Story of th American War of Independence. By Eliza F. Pollard.

Great Works by Great Men: The Story c Famous Engineers and their Triumphs. By F. M. Holmes.

Lady of the Forest (The). By L. T. Meade Author of " Scamp and I," " Sweet Nancy," etc.

Lion City of Africa (The): A Story of Adventure By Willis Boyd Allen, Author of "The Red Mountain of Alaska," etc.

Mark Seaworth: A Tale of the Indian Archipelago By W. H. G. Kingston, Author of " Manco, the Peruvian Chief."

Manco, The Peruvian Chief. By W. H. G Kingston. New Edition. Illustrated by Lancelot Speed.

Roger the Ranger: A Story of Border Life amon the Indians. By Eliza F. Pollard, Author of " Not Wanted," etc.

Red Mountain of Alaska (The). By Willis Boy Allen, Author of " Pine Cones," " The Northern Cross," etc.

True unto Death: A Story of Russian Life and th Crimean War. By Eliza F. Pollard, Author of " Roger the Ranger.

White Dove of Amritzir (The): A Romance c Anglo-Indian Life. By Eliza F. Pollard.

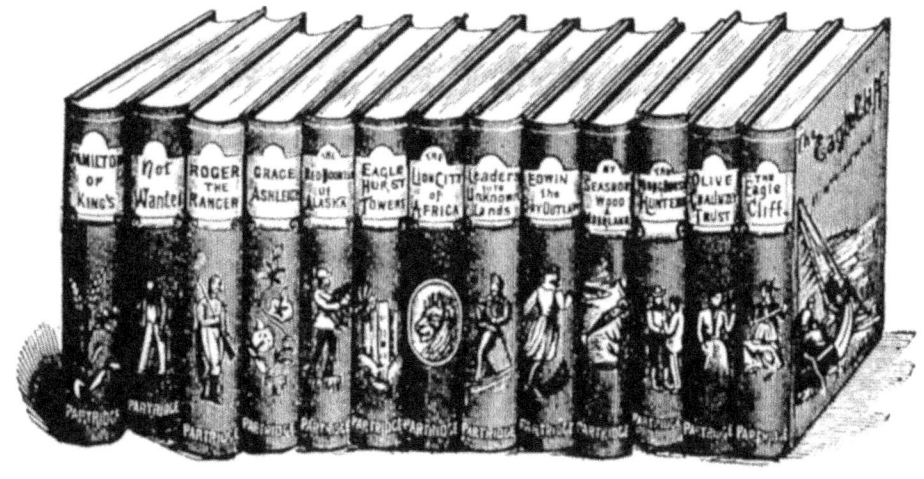

THE HOME LIBRARY.

Crown 8vo. 320 pages. Handsome Cloth Covers. Illustrations. 2s. each.

From "Aveline's Inheritance."

Aveline's Inheritance. By
Jennie Chappell. Illustrated. Cloth boards.

In bright vivacious style the author narrates how a fortune passed from one to another until it reached the rightful heir. Aveline, the heroine, is a vigorous Christian character, and how she nobly uses her inheritance for the benefit of her less fortunate brother forms a fitting conclusion to a stimulating and healthy book.

Around the Fire: Yule-tide
Stories. By M. S. Haycraft. Illustrated. Crown 8vo, cloth boards.

The Spanish Maiden: A
Story of Brazil. By Emma E. Hornibrook.

Grace Ashleigh; or, His
Ways are Best. By Mary D. R. Boyd. 320 pages. Eight illustrations.

The story of a consecrated life and earnest endeavour to glorify God in the midst of opposition and difficulty.

Fortune's Wheel. By Eliza F. Pollard.
An interesting story of South African life, and of evil overcome by good.

Martyr of Kolin (The): The Story of the Bohemian
Persecution. By H. O. Ward.

"Conveys a strong impression of reality, and is eminently fitted to foster a love for religious liberty, more especially in the young."—*Aberdeen Free Press.*

A Village Story. By Mrs. G. E. Morton. Author of
"The Story of Jesus," "A Trio of Cousins," "Foreshadowed," etc.

A book of more than ordinary interest. Deeply spiritual in tone: A valuable contribution to the literature suited for Sunday School Prizes and Libraries.

Clouds that Pass. By E. Gertrude Hart.

Child of Genius (A). By Lily Watson.

Wardlaugh; or, Workers To-
gether. By Charlotte Murray.

A story of earnest Christian work in a Scottish village. Bright and helpful.

Out of the Deep. By E.
Harcourt Burrage.

Miss Elizabeth's Niece.
By M. S. Haycraft.

More Precious than Gold.
By Jennie Chappell.

John Halifax, Gentleman.
By Mrs. Craik. New Edition. 540 pages.

Ben-Hur. By L. Wallace.

From "The Martyr of Kolin."

6

THE HOME LIBRARY—*(continued)*.

Better Part (The). By Annie S. Swan.

Bunch of Cherries (A). By J. W. Kirton.

Cousin Mary. By Mrs. Oliphant, Author of "Chronicles of Carlingford," etc.

Dr. Cross ; or, Tried and True. By Ruth Sterling.

Dorothy's Training ; or, Wild-Flower or Weed? By Jennie Chappell.

Gerard Mastyn ; or, The Son of a Genius. By E. Harcourt Burrage.

Honor : a Nineteenth Century Heroine. By E. M. Alford.

Her Saddest Blessing. By Jennie Chappell.

John : A Tale of the Messiah. By K. Pearson Woods.

Living It Down. By Laura M. Lane.

Morning Dew-Drops. By Clara Lucas Balfour.

Mark Desborough's Vow. By Annie S. Swan.

Mick Tracy, the Irish Scripture Reader. By the Author of "Tim Doolan, the Irish Emigrant."

Naomi; or, The Last Days of Jerusalem. By Mrs. Webb.

Pilgrim's Progress (The). By John Bunyan. 416 pages. 47 Illustrations.

Petrel Darcy ; or, In Honour Bound. By T. Corrie.

Strait Gate (The). By Annie S. Swan.

Polar Eden (A): or, The Goal of the "Dauntless." By Charles R. Kenyon, Author of "The Young Ranchman," etc.

Uncle Tom's Cabin. By Harriet Beecher Stowe.

Without a Thought ; or, Dora's Discipline. By Jennie Chappell.

Nearly 400,000 of these volumes have already been sold.

2s. each.

Bible Light for Little Pilgrims.
A Coloured Scripture Picture Roll, containing Twelve beautifully Coloured Old and New Testament Scenes, with appropriate texts. Varnished cover, printed in ten colours. Mounted on roller for hanging. 2s.

Bible Picture Roll.
Containing a large Engraving of a Scripture Subject, with letterpress for each day in the month. Mounted on roller. 2s.

The Friends of Jesus.
Illustrated Sketches for the Young, of the Twelve Apostles, the Family at Bethany, and other of the earthly friends of the Saviour. Small 4to. Cloth extra. 2s.

Domestic Pets:
Their Habits and Treatment. Anecdotal and Descriptive. Full of Illustrations. Fcap. 4to. Cloth extra. 2s

1s. 6d. each.

NEW SERIES OF MISSIONARY BIOGRAPHIES.

Crown 8vo. 160 pages. Cloth extra. Fully Illustrated. 1s. 6d. each.

James Chalmers, Missionary and Explorer
of Raratonga and New Guinea. By William Robson. New Edition, brought up-to-date by Frank B. Broad, of the London Missionary Society.

Griffith John, Founder of the Hankow Mission,
Central China. By William Robson. New Edition, brought up-to-date by Frank B. Broad.

Amid Greenland Snows; or, The Early
History of Arctic Missions.

Bishop Patteson, the Martyr of
Melanesia.

By Jesse Page.

Captain Allen Gardiner:
Sailor and Saint. By Jesse Page, Author of " Japan, its People and Missions," etc.

Congo for Christ (The) The Story of the Congo
Mission. By Rev. J. B. Myers, Author of " William Carey, ' etc.

David Brainerd, the Apostle to the North
American Indians. By Jesse Page.

Japan: Its People and Missions. By Jesse Page.

John Williams, the Martyr Missionary of
Polynesia. By Rev. James J. Ellis.

James Calvert; or, From Dark to Dawn in Fiji. By
R. Vernon.

Lady Missionaries in Foreign Lands. By
Mrs. E. R. Pitman, Author of " Vestina's Martyrdom," etc.

Madagascar: Its Missionaries and Martyrs.
By William J. Townsend, Author of " Robert Morrison," etc.

Missionary Heroines in Eastern Lands. By
Mrs. E. R. Pitman, Author of " Lady Missionaries in Foreign Lands."

Robert Moffat, the Missionary Hero of
Kuruman. By David J. Deane.

Robert Morrison, the Pioneer of Chinese
Missions. By William John Townsend, General Secretary of the
Methodist New Connexion Missionary Society.

Samuel Crowther, the Slave Boy who
became Bishop of the Niger. By Jesse Page.

Thomas J. Comber, Missionary Pioneer to
the Congo. By Rev. J. B. Myers, Association Secretary, Baptist
Missionary Society.

From Kafir Kraal to the Pulpit: The Story of
Tiyo Soga, first ordained preacher of the Kafir Race.

William Carey, the Shoemaker who became
the Father and Founder of Modern Missions. By Rev. J. B.
Myers.

NEW POPULAR BIOGRAPHIES.

Crown 8vo. 160 pages. Maps and Illustrations. Cloth extra. 1s. *6d. each.*

Dwight L. Moody: The Life-work of a Modern Evan-
gelist. By Rev. J. H. Batt.

Noble Work by Noble Women: Sketches of the
lives of the Baroness Burdett-Coutts, Lady Henry Somerset, Miss
Robinson, Mrs. Fawcett, and Mrs. Gladstone. By Jennie Chappell,
Author of " Four Noble Women," etc.

Four Noble Women and their Work: Sketches
of the Life and Work of Frances Willard, Agnes Weston, Sister Dora,
and Catherine Booth. By Jennie Chappell.

Canal Boy who became President (The).
By Frederic T. Gammon. Twelfth Edition. Thirty-fourth Thousand.

David Livingstone: His Labours and His Legacy.
By Arthur Montefiore-Brice, F.R.G.S.

Florence Nightingale, the Wounded Soldier's Friend. By Eliza F. Pollard.

Four Heroes of India: Clive, Warren Hastings, Havelock, Lawrence. By F. M. Holmes.

Fridtjof Nansen: His Life and Explorations. By J. Arthur Bain.

General Gordon, the Christian Soldier and Hero. By G. Barnett Smith.

Gladstone (W. E.): Eng-land's Great Commoner. By Walter Jerrold. With Portrait and Thirty-eight other Illustrations.

Heroes and Heroines of the Scottish Covenanters. By J. Meldrum Dryerre, LL.B., F.R.G.S.

From " Florence Nightingale."

John Knox and the Scottish Reformation. By G. Barnett Smith.

Michael Faraday, Man of Science. By Walter Jerrold.

Philip Melancthon, the Wittemberg Pro-fessor and Theologian of the Reformation. By David J. Deane, Author of " Two Noble Lives," etc.

Sir Richard Tangye (" One and All "). An Auto-biography. With Twenty-one Original Illustrations by Frank Hewitt. (192 pages.)

Sir John Franklin and the Romance of the North-West Passage. By G. Barnett Smith.

Stanley (Henry M.), the African Explorer. By Arthur Montefiore-Brice, F.R.G.S.

Spurgeon (C. H.): His Life and Ministry. By Jesse Page.

Two Noble Lives: JOHN WICLIFFE, the Morning Star of the Reformation; and MARTIN LUTHER, the Reformer. By David J. Deane. (208 pages.)

William Tyndale, the Translator of the English Bible. By G. Barnett Smith.

Alexander Maclaren: The Man and His Message. A Character Sketch. By John E. Carlile, Author of " The Royal Life." 1s. 6d. *net.*

Joseph Parker, D.D.: His Life and Ministry. By Albert Dawson. Crown 8vo. 160 pages. Illustrated. Cloth boards. 1s. 6d. *net.*

General Booth: The Man and His Work. By Jesse Page. Crown 8vo. 160 pages. Illustrated. Cloth boards. 1s. 6d. *net.*

Hugh Price Hughes. By Rev. J. Gregory Mantle. 160 pages. Illustrated. Cloth boards. 1s. 6d. *net.*

1s. 6d. each.

Triumphs of the Printing Press. By Walter Jerrold.

Astronomers and their Observations. By Lucy Taylor. With Preface by W. Thynne Lynn, B.A., F.R.A.S.

Celebrated Mechanics and their Achievements. By F. M. Holmes.

Chemists and their Wonders. By F. M. Holmes.

Engineers and their Triumphs. By F. M. Holmes.

Electricians and their Marvels. By Walter Jerrold.

Musicians and their Compositions. By J. R. Griffiths.

Naturalists and their Investigations. By George Day, F.R.M.S.

THE BRITISH BOYS' LIBRARY.

A New Series of 1s. 6d. *Books for Boys. Illustrated. Crown 8vo. Cloth extra.*

From " Heroes All! "

Heroes All! A Book of Brave Deeds for British Boys. Edited by C. D. Michael, Author of " Deeds of Daring," etc.

Deeds of Daring; or, Stories of Heroism in Every-day Life. Selected by C. D. Michael, Author of " Noble Deeds," etc.

The Thane of the Dean. By Tom Bevan, Author of " White Ivory and Black."

Noble Deeds: A Book of Stories of Peril and Heroism. By Charles D. Michael.

Armour Bright. By Lucy Taylor.

The Old Red School House: A Story of the Backwoods. By Frances H. Wood.

Ben: A Story of Life's Byways. By Lydia Phillips, Author of "Frank Burleigh."

Major Brown; or, Whether White or Black, a Man. By Edith S. Davis.

The Bell Buoy; or, The Story of a Mysterious Key. By F. M. Holmes.

Jack: A Story of a Scapegrace. By E. M. Bryant.

Hubert Ellerdale: A Tale of the Days of Wicliffe. By W. Oak Rhind.

THE BRITISH GIRLS' LIBRARY.

A New Series of 1s. 6d. Books for Girls. Illustrated. Crown 8vo. Cloth extra.

Lady of Greyham (The); or, Low in a Low Place. By Emma E. Hornibrook.

Gipsy Queen (The). By Emma Leslie.

Kathleen ; or, A Maiden's Influence. By Julia Hack.

Crystal Joyce : The Story of a Golden Life. By Edward Garrett.

Christabel's Influence. By J. Goldsmith Cooper, Author of "Nella."

Maid of the Storm (The) : A Story of a Cornish Village. By Nellie Cornwall.

Queen of the Isles. By Jessie M. E. Saxby.

NEW PICTURE BOOKS.

Pleasures and Joys for Girls and Boys. By D. J. D., Author of "Anecdotes of Animal Sagacity." With 8 coloured and 111 other Illustrations. Size 9 by 7 inches. Handsome coloured cover, paper boards and cloth back. 1s. 6d.

Happy and Gay : Pictures and Stories for Every Day. By D. J. D., Author of "Stories of Animal Sagacity," etc. With 8 coloured and 97 other Illustrations. Size 9 by 7 inches. Handsome coloured cover, paper boards with cloth backs. 1s. 6d.

Anecdotes of Animals and Birds. By Uncle John. With 57 full-page and other Illustrations by Harrison Weir, etc. F'cap. 4to. 128 pages. Handsomely bound in paper boards, with Animal design in 10 colours, varnished. 1s. 6d.

Stories of Animal Sagacity. By D. J. D. A companion volume to "Anecdotes of Animals." Numerous full-page Illustrations. Handsomely bound in paper boards, with Animal subject printed in 10 colours, varnished. 1s. 6d.

ILLUSTRATED REWARD BOOKS.

Crown 8vo. 160 pages. Cloth extra. Fully Illustrated. 1s. 6d. each.

From " Little Soldiers."

Little Soldiers. By Kate L. Mackley.

The Golden Doors. By M. S. Haycraft.

A Late Repentance. By Hannah B. Mackenzie, Author of " Crowned Victor," etc.

Will; or, " That Boy from the Union." By L. Phillips, Author of " Frank Burleigh," etc.

A Red Brick Cottage. By Lady Hope, Author of " His Handywork," etc.

Shepherds and Sheep. By E. Stuart-Langford, Author of " A Measuring Eye," etc.

Our Phyllis. By M. S. Haycraft, Author of " Sister Royal," etc.

Chrissie's Endeavour.
Three People. } By " Pansy."

The Young Moose Hunters. By C. A. Stephens.

Eaglehurst Towers. By Emma Marshall.

A Measuring Eye. By E. Stuart-Langford, Author of " Miss Sophia's Repentance," etc.

Aileen; or, " The Love of Christ Constraineth Us." By Laura A. Barter, Author of " Harold ; or, Two Died for Me."

Duff Darlington ; or, " An Unsuspected Genius." By Evelyn Everett-Green.

Everybody's Friend ; or, Hilda Danvers' Influence. By Evelyn Everett-Green.

Fine Gold ; or, Ravenswood Courtenay. By Emma Marshall, Author of " Eaglehurst Towers," etc.

Hiram Golf's Religion. By Geo. H. Hepworth, D.D.

In Friendship's Name : A Story for Boys. By L. Phillips, Author of " Frank Burleigh," etc.

Marchester Stories. By Rev. Charles Herbert. Illustrated. Crown 8vo. Cloth boards.

Nella ; or, Not My Own. By Jessie Goldsmith Cooper.

The Legend of the Silver Cup : Allegories for Children. By Rev. G. Critchley, B.A. (Small quarto.)

From " Will ; or, ' That Boy from the Union.' "

Our Duty to Animals. By Mrs. C. Bray, Author of "Physiology for Schools," etc. Intended to teach the young kindness to animals. Cloth 1s. 6d.; School Edition, 1s. 3d.

Raymond and Bertha: A Story of True Nobility. By L. Phillips, Author of "Frank Burleigh."

Rose Capel's Sacrifice; or, A Mother's Love. By Mrs. Haycraft, Author of "Like a Little Candle."

Satisfied. By Catherine M. Trowbridge.

Ted's Trust; or, Aunt Elmerley's Umbrella. By Jennie Chappell, Author of "Who was the Culprit?" etc.

Tamsin Rosewarne and Her Burdens: A Tale of Cornish Life. By Nellie Cornwall.

1s. each.

ONE SHILLING REWARD BOOKS.

Fully Illustrated. Crown 8vo. Cloth extra. 1s. each.

From "All Play and No Work."

All Play and No Work. By Harold Avery, Author of "The Triple Alliance," etc.

Bernard or Ben? By Jennie Chappell, Author of "Raymond's Rival," etc.

Paul the Courageous. By Mabel Quiller-Couch, Author of "Some Western Folk," etc.

Uncle Zeph and his Yarns. By W. J. Forster.

Raymond's Angel: A Story of Two Lives Laid Down. By Blanche Garvock.

Lost in the Backwoods. By Edith C. Kenyon, Author of "Brave Bertie," etc.

Roy's Sister. By M. B. Manwell.

Cola Monti; or, The Story of a Genius. By Mrs. Craik, Author of "John Halifax, Gentleman."

Bessie Drew; or, The Odd Little Girl. By Amy Manifold.

Dumpy Dolly. By E. M. Waterworth, Author of Master Lionel," "Lady Betty's Twins," etc.

A Venturesome Voyage. By F. Scarlet Potter, Author of "The Farm by the Wood," etc.

The Pilgrim's Progress. By John Bunyan. 416 pages. 47 Illustrations.

Always Happy; or, The Story of Helen Keller. By Jennie Chappell, Author of "Ted's Trust."

From " Paul the Courageous."

Birdie and Her Dog. By E. C. Phillips.

Children of Cherryholme (The). By M. S Haycraft, Author of " Like a Little Candle," " Chine Cabin," etc.

Farm by the Wood (The). By F. Scarlett Potter, Author of " Phil's Frolic," etc.

Frank Burleigh; or, Chosen to be a Soldier. By L. Phillips.

His Majesty's Beggars. By Mary E. Ropes, Author of " Bel's Baby," etc.

Harold; or, Two Died for Me. By Laura A. Barter.

Indian Life in the Great North-West. By Egerton R. Young, Missionary to the North American Indian tribes, North of Lake Winnipeg, Author of " By Canoe and Dog Train," etc.

Jack the Conqueror; or, Difficulties Overcome. By the Author of " Dick and his Donkey."

Jim's Discovery; or, On the Edge of a Desert. By T. M. Browne, Author of " Dawson's Madge," etc.

Little Bunch's Charge; or, True to Trust. By Nellie Cornwall, Author of " Tamsin Rosewarne," etc.

Little Woodman and his Dog Cæsar (The). By Mrs. Sherwood.

Marjory; or, What Would Jesus Do? By Laura A. Barter, Author of " Harold; or, Two Died for Me."

Our Den. By E. M. Waterworth, Author of " Master Lionel, that Tiresome Child."

Raymond's Rival; or, Which will Win? By Jennie Chappell, Author of " Losing and Finding," etc.

Sweet Nancy. By L. T. Meade, Author of " Scamp and I," " A Band of Three," etc.

Twice Saved; or, Somebody's Pet and Nobody's Darling. By E. M. Waterworth, Author of " Our Den," " Master Lionel," etc.

Who was the Culprit? By Jennie Chappell, Author of " Her Saddest Blessing," " The Man of the Family," etc.

ONE SHILLING PICTURE BOOKS.

Size, 10½ by 8 inches. Bound in handsome Coloured Paper Boards, with Coloured and other Illustrations. 1s. each.

Our Pets' Picture Book. By D. J. D., Author of " A Merry Game," etc.

Happy Playmates : Pictures and Stories for Young Folks. By J. D , Author of " Buttercups and Daisies," etc.

Bible Pictures and Stories. Old Testament. **By** D. J. D.

Bible Pictures and Stories. New Testament. **By** James Weston and D. J. D.

Pussies and Puppies. By Louis Wain.

A Merry Game : Pictures and Stories for Little Readers. By D. J. D., Author of " Dapple and Dobbin's Picture Book," etc.

Dapple and Dobbin's Picture Book. By D. J. D., Author, of " Happy and Gay," etc.

Buttercups and Daisies : A Picture Story Book for Little People. By J. D. Size 9 by 7¼ inches.

Holiday Hours in Animal Land. By Uncle Harry. New Edition. 96 pages. Size, 9 by 7¼ inches.

Skipping Time : A Story Book in Prose and Rhyme. By C. D. M., Author of " Holiday Joys," etc. Size, 9 by 7¼ inches.

Ring o' Roses : Pictures and Stories for Little Folks. By Uncle Jack, Author of " Frolic and Fun," etc. Fcap. quarto.

Holiday Joys : Stories and Pictures for Girls and Boys. By C. D. M., Author of " Merry Playmates," etc. Fcap. quarto.

Father Time. A novel mechanical Toy Book. With Cover beautifully printed in Colours, and Clock face with movable hands. Size, 11 by 9 inches.

CHEAP REPRINTS OF POPULAR STORIES FOR THE YOUNG.

Crown 8vo. 160 pages. Illustrated. Cloth Boards. 1s. each.

Her Two Sons. A Story for Young Men and Maidens. By Mrs. Charles Garnett.

Marigold. By L. T. Meade, Author of "The Lady of the Forest," etc.

Jack's Heroism : A Tale of Schoolboy Life. By E. C. Kenyon, Author of "Lost in the Backwoods," etc.

Rag and Tag : A Plea for the Waifs and Strays of Old England. By Mrs. E. J. Whittaker.

From "Like a Little Candle."

Through Life's Shadows. By Eliza F. Pollard.

The Little Princess of Tower Hill. By L. T. Meade.

Clovie and Madge. By Mrs. G. S. Reaney.

Bible Jewels. By Dr. Newton.

Bible Wonders. By the same Author.

Rills from the Fountain of Life. By the same Author.

Ellerslie House : A Book for Boys. By Emma Leslie.

Like a Little Candle ; or, Bertrand's Influence. By Mrs. Haycraft.

The Lads of Kingston : A Tale of a Seaport Town. By James Capes Story.

Violet Maitland ; or, By Thorny Ways. By Laura M. Lane.

Martin Redfern's Oath. By Ethel F. Heddle.

Dairyman's Daughter (The). By Legh Richmond.

Victoria ; The Well-Beloved (1819-1901). By W. Francis Aitkin. Crown 8vo. 152 pages. Eight Illustrations Cloth boards. 1s.

Keynotes to the Happy Life. By Mrs. Charles Skinner, Author of "For Love's Sake," etc. Demy 16mo. Cloth boards. 1s.

For Love's Sake. By Mrs. Charlotte Skinner. Demy 16mo. Cloth boards, 1s.

Uncrowned Queens. By Mrs. Charlotte Skinner, Author of "Sisters of the Master." Small 8vo. 112 pages. Cloth. 1s.

Sisters of the Master. By Mrs. Charlotte Skinner, Author of "The Master's Gifts to Women." Small 8vo., cloth. 1s.

The Master's Messages to Women. By Mrs. Charlotte Skinner. Small 8vo., cloth. 1s.

Some Secrets of Christian Living. Selections from the "Seven Rules" Series of Booklets. Small 8vo., cloth. 1s.

Steps to the Blessed Life. Selections from the "Seven Rules" Series of Booklets. By Rev. F. B. Meyer, B.A. Small Crown 8vo. Cloth boards. 1s.

Thoroughness : Talks to Young Men. By Thain Davidson, D.D. Small Crown 8vo. Cloth extra. 1s.

Molly and I. By the Author of "Jack," "At Sunset," etc. Long 8vo. Illustrated Title Page. Cloth extra. 1s.

Cicely's Little Minute. By Harvey Gobel. Long 8vo. Illustrated Title Page. Cloth extra. 1s.

Won from the Sea. By E. C. Phillips, Author of "Birdie and her Dog."

From "Won from the Sea."

Aunt Armstrong's Money. By Jennie Chappell, Author of "Carol's Gift," etc.

John Blessington's Enemy. A Story of Life in South Africa. By E. Harcourt Burrage, Author of "The Fatal Nugget," etc.

Carol's Gift ; or, "What Time I am Afraid I will Trust in Thee." By Jennie Chappell.

Cripple George ; or, God has a Plan for every Man: A Temperance Story. By John W. Kneeshaw, Author of "Norcliffe Court," etc.

Cared for ; or, The Orphan Wanderers. By Mrs. C. E. Bowen, Author of "Dick and his Donkey," etc.

NINEPENNY SERIES OF ILLUSTRATED BOOKS—*(continued)*.

Rob and I; or, By Courage and Faith. By C. A. Mercer.

Phil's Frolic. By F. Scarlett Potter.

How a Farthing made a Fortune; or, Honesty is the Best Policy. By Mrs. C. E. Bowen.

A Flight with the Swallows. By Emma Marshall.

Babes in the Basket (The); or, Daph and Her Charge.

Bel's Baby. By Mary E. Ropes.

Benjamin Holt's Boys, and What They Did for Him. By the Author of "A Candle Lighted by the Lord."

Birdie's Benefits; or, "A Little Child Shall Lead Them." By Ethel Ruth Boddy.

Five Cousins (The). By Emma Leslie.

Foolish Chrissy; or, Discontent and its Consequences. By Meta, Author of "Noel's Lesson," etc.

For Lucy's Sake. By Annie S. Swan.

Giddie Garland; or, The Three Mirrors. By Jennie Chappell.

How Paul's Penny became a Pound. By Mrs. Bowen, Author of "Dick and His Donkey."

How Peter's Pound became a Penny. By the same Author.

John Oriel's Start in Life. By Mary Howitt.

Master Lionel, that Tiresome Child. By E. M. Waterworth.

Man of the Family (The). By Jennie Chappell.

Mattie's Home; or, The Little Match-girl and her Friends.

Paul, a Little Mediator. By Maude M. Butler.

Sailor's Lass (A). By Emma Leslie.

Una Bruce's Troubles. By Alice Price. Illustrated by Harold Copping.

NEW SERIES OF SIXPENNY PICTURE-BOOKS.

Crown quarto. Fully Illustrated. Handsomely bound in paper boards, with design printed in Ten colours. 6d. each.

Sweet Blossom : A Picture Story Book for Little Ones.

Sweet Stories Retold : A Bible Picture Book for Young Folks.

Going A-Sailing : A Picture Story Book for Little Folks.

Off to Toyland : Pictures and Stories for Little People.

Under the Oak Tree : Pictures and Stories for Little Ones.

Tibby's Tales : A Picture Book for Little People.

Dollies' Schooltime : Pictures and Stories in Prose and Rhyme.

Birdie's Message : The Little Folks' Picture Book.

This New Series of Picture Books surpasses, in excellence of illustration and careful printing, all others at the price.

NEW COLOURED SCRIPTURE PICTURE-BOOKS.

Beautifully printed in Chromo-Lithography. Size 8½ by 6 inches. Stiff Paper Coloured Covers, with Cloth Backs, 6d. each.

Coming to Jesus : Texts, Verses, and Coloured Pictures.

The Good Shepherd : Texts, Verses, and Coloured Pictures.

THE "RED DAVE" SERIES.

New and Enlarged Edition. Illustrated. Handsomely bound in cloth boards. 6d. each.

Benjamin's New Boy. By Jesse Page.

Enemies: A Tale for Little Lads and Lasses. By Marion Isabel Hurrell.

Cherry Tree Place. By Lizzie A. Hooper.

A Tale of Four Foxes. By Eva C. Rogers.

A Little Town Mouse. By Eleanora H. Stooke.

Left In Charge, and other Stories.

A Threefold Promise.

Two Little Girls, and What they Did.

The Four Young Musicians.

Joe and Sally; or, A Good Deed and its Fruits.

The Island Home. By F. M. Holmes.

Chrissy's Treasure. By Jennie Perrett.

Puppy-Dog Tales. By various Authors.

Mother's Boy. By M. B. Manwell.

A Great Mistake. By Jennie Chappell.

From Hand to Hand. By C. J. Hamilton.

That Boy Bob. By Jesse Page.

Buy Your Own Cherries. By J. W. Kirton.

Owen's Fortune. By Mrs. F. West.

Shad's Christmas Gift.

Red Dave; or, What Wilt Thou have Me to do.

Dick and his Donkey; or, How to Pay the Rent.

Lost in the Snow; or, The Kentish Fisherman.

Jessie Dyson.

Maude's Visit to Sandy-beach.

Come Home, Mother.

4d. each.

THE YOUNG FOLKS' LIBRARY.

of Cloth-bound Books for the Young. With Coloured Frontispieces. 64 pages. Well Illustrated. Handsome Cloth Covers. 4d. each.

Ronald's Reason.

Shadow to Shine.

A Bright Idea.

The Little Woodman.

Jacko the Monkey, and other Stories.

Little Dan, the Orange Boy.

The Church Mouse.

Sybil.

Dandy Jim.

A Troublesome Trio.

Perry's Pilgrimage.

Nita; or, Among the Brigands.

CHEAP "PANSY" SERIES.

Imperial 8vo. 64 pages. Many Illustrations. Cover printed in Five Colours. 4d. each.

The Better Part. By Annie S. Swan.

The Household Angel. By Madeline Leslie.

The Strait Gate. By Annie S. Swan.

Mark Desborough's Vow. By Annie S. Swan.

Her Saddest Blessing.

Miss Priscilla Hunter, and other Stories.

Wild Bryonie.

Avice : A Story of Imperial Rome.

From Different Standpoints.

Those Boys.

The Chautauqua Girls at Home.

Christie's Christmas.

Wise to Win ; or, the Master Hand.

Ester Ried.

Julia Ried.

Ester Ried yet Speaking.

An Endless Chain.

Echoing and Re-echoing.

Cunning Workmen.

Tip Lewis and His Lamp.

The King's Daughter.

Household Puzzles.

The Randolphs.

Links in Rebecca's Life.

A New Graft on the Family Tree.

The Man of the House.

THE TINY LIBRARY.

Books printed in large type. Cloth boards. 3d. each.

Little Chrissie, and other Stories.

Harry Carlton's Holiday.

A Little Loss and a Big Find.

What a Little Cripple Did.

Bobby.

Matty and Tom.

The Broken Window.

John Madge's Cure for Selfishness.

The Pedlar's Loan.

Letty Young's Trials.

Brave Boys.

Little Jem, the Rag Merchant.

NEW SERIES OF THREEPENNY PICTURE BOOKS.

Royal 16mo. Coloured Frontispiece and numerous other Illustrations. Bound in paper boards with cloth back, with Cover beautifully printed in Colours. 3d. each.

By the Sea.

"Pets" and "Pickles.'

Toby and Kit's Animal Book.

Our Little Pets' Alphabet.

Bible Stories. Old Testament.

Bible Stories. New Testament

ILLUSTRATED MONTHLY PERIODICALS.

THE BRITISH WORKMAN.
ONE PENNY MONTHLY.

An Illustrated Paper containing Popular Articles and Stories on Temperance, Thrift, etc., and short Biographies of eminent Self-made Men : also interesting accounts of visits to some of our leading British Industries.

The Yearly Volume, with coloured paper boards, cloth back, and full of Engravings, 1s. 6d. ; cloth, 2s. 6d.

THE BAND OF HOPE REVIEW.
ONE HALFPENNY MONTHLY.

The Leading Temperance Periodical for the Young, containing Serial and Short Stories, Concerted Recitations, Prize Competitions, etc. Should be in the hands of all Members of the Bands of Hope.

The Yearly Volume, with coloured paper boards and cloth back, full of Engravings, 1s. ; cloth boards, 1s. 6d.

THE CHILDREN'S FRIEND.
ONE PENNY MONTHLY.

Charming Stories, interesting Articles, Indoor Recreations, beautiful Pictures, Puzzles, Music, Prize Competitions, etc.

The Yearly Volume, coloured paper boards, cloth back, 1s. 6d. ; cloth, 2s. ; gilt edges, 2s. 6d.

THE FAMILY FRIEND.
ONE PENNY MONTHLY.

A beautifully Illustrated Magazine for the Home Circle, with Serial and Short Stories by popular Authors, Helpful Articles, Hints on Dressmaking, Music, etc.

The Yearly Volume, with numerous Engravings, coloured paper boards, cloth back, 1s. 6d. ; cloth, 2s. ; gilt edges, 2s. 6d.

THE INFANTS' MAGAZINE.
ONE PENNY MONTHLY.

No other Periodical can be compared with the Infants' Magazine for freshness, brightness and interest. Full of Bright Pictures and pleasant reading to delight the little ones.

The Yearly Volume, in coloured paper boards, cloth back, 1s. 6d. ; cloth, 2s. ; gilt edges, 2s. 6d.

THE FRIENDLY VISITOR.
AN ILLUSTRATED GOSPEL MAGAZINE FOR THE PEOPLE.
ONE PENNY MONTHLY.

Full of entertaining reading with sound religious teaching in the form of story, article and poem. Printed in large type and fully Illustrated. Just the paper for the aged.

The Yearly Volume, coloured paper boards, cloth back, 1s. 6d. cloth, 2s. ; gilt edges, 2s. 6d.

8 & 9, PATERNOSTER ROW, E.C.